TWISTED CAPTIVE

PATRICIA D. EDDY

CHAPTER ONE

AURELIA

The sweet scent of willow bark fills the air as I carry my large basket of freshly dyed wool blankets, socks, and shawls to the town square. The market begins soon, and today's offerings should allow me to earn enough to buy food and goods to last another three or four weeks.

My fingers ache as I adjust my grip. Sheering season always brings extra work, and I'm glad for it, even if I do wish my father could help me with the spinning like he used to. But he's given in to despair the past few years, and loses himself to the drink too often.

All around me, others make their way to their assigned stalls, some laboring under the weight of sackfuls of potatoes, apples, or grain, others less burdened with spices or dried goods.

"Good morning, Aurelia." Roarke's deep voice sends a little thrill through me as he eases my basket from my arms and carries it the last few paces to my stall. "Let me assist you."

My cheeks flush bright pink—at least I imagine they do—and I struggle to form words. "I...it's not your place...I mean..."

His golden eyes find mine. "We are equals, Aurelia."

"We are not." I stare down at my hands. My fingertips are calloused, my joints swollen and sore. It is my penance for being born without magic. For being the *daughter* of one born without magic.

This realm has two types of people. The magical and the outcasts. We are the outcasts. Roarke? He has magic within him. Enough to keep him in the good graces of those who keep us trapped here. The Fae.

"Here," he traces a knuckle over the heart-shaped neckline of my corset, close to my heart, "we are."

I can't help leaning in when he does. Our lips are only a whisper apart, and I think, perhaps, this is the day he'll finally kiss me as I have always wanted to be kissed.

For over a year, we have bantered back and forth on Market days, and he even came to the cottage for supper with us a few months back. But that night ended badly when my father had too much mulled wine and screamed that he would never let a magic-bearer court his daughter. I thought Roarke would never speak to me again.

I was wrong. Still, he pursues me. Steals moments of closeness, holds my hand, kisses my cheek. "Roarke, what do you want from me?" I ask, peering up into his hazel eyes where the gold streaks flare brightly.

"Your trust, darling. Perhaps one day, your heart. If you choose to give it. I adore you, Aurelia. I have from the moment we first met. If only you believed me."

Any reply stalls on my lips as my heartbeat quickens. I wish I could allow myself to love him. But the laws of this realm forbid it, and if the Fae discovered our desire for one another, they would not punish Roarke. No. They would punish me.

A commotion breaks out at the edge of the square. A fight between the mulled wine vendor and the beer peddler. Those two are always going at it, and if they are not careful, the Fae will come down from the stone castle that towers above the town and put an end to both of them.

Roarke's eyes widen, and he hurries towards the fray. With a hard shove, he sends Brall, the wine vendor, stumbling back. Javer grabs one of his bottles of dark brew and brandishes it over his head. "You stole your recipes from *my father*," he says as he tries to get past Roarke to Brall.

"I did no such thing." Brall pushes to his feet and brushes off his black pants and waistcoat. "My recipes are my own."

Roarke wrestles the bottle from Javer's hand and sets it back down on his table. "Enough of this. Do you not see the position of the sun? It is close to its peak, and the Fae will soon walk among us. If they find you fighting, your lives will be forfeit."

The two grumble, but go back to their respective booths and start arranging their wares.

A glance at the sky sends my heart into my throat. I dawdled for too long wishing for things I can never have. All of my blankets, socks, and cloaks should be properly displayed by now.

My hands tremble as I pull each item from my basket and drape it over the racks affixed to the sides of my tent. Securing my coin purse around my waist, I smooth down my skirt and wait for the market bell to toll. Already, the locals who do not have wares to sell are milling about, planning their purchases.

And Roarke? I can no longer see him. With a sigh, I scuff at the cobblestones with the toe of my well-worn boot. We are not meant to be. I know this. And even if we were, the Fae would never allow our union.

Outcasts can only marry outcasts. And that's all I will ever be.

~

ROARKE

Market day is pure torture for me. I have to watch those with magic—those like me—treat Aurelia like she is less than human. They insist she lower her prices for the wools she spins and dyes by hand, call her names, or ignore her completely. I have paid everyone I trust over the years to purchase something from her—for full price of course—and soon, I do not know what I will be able to do for her if she does not allow me to court her properly.

This realm is cursed. Nearly two centuries ago, the King was exiled from the Fae realm and forced to live among humans. But he abhors those who are not Fae, and instead found a way to create his own realm here in Greenland. I do not know how he was strong enough to do this, but the barrier is inescapable.

Those who venture too close to the veil are transported to the center of the realm, directly in front of the castle, and then judged as either magic bearers or outcasts. Seventy-five years ago, my dragon flew directly into the veil, and I was fortunate that the shock of the magic caused me to shift back into a man. A very naked man.

How the Fae King did not sense the shifter within me, I do not know.

"Look at him," the King says to one of his guards. *"What kind of idiot do you need to be to be running across the lands without clothing?"*

I kneel. Not by choice, but because his influence forces me to my knees and I am too disoriented to fight back.

"What is your name?" the King asks.

"Roarke," I answer.

With a few words in Gaelic, the King uses his air charms to steal my breath, and I clutch at my throat. My own magic fights to escape, but I force my mind to blank—as much as I can—so my thoughts cannot betray me.

"You are a magic bearer," the King says as he releases the charm and I wheeze.

Three guards advance on me, and as their fists rain down over my back and torso, the King chuckles. "How delicious. Listen carefully, Roarke. This realm is mine, and those with magic enjoy many privileges. Provided you transfer some of that magic every single day into the Ley lines. Do that, and you will be rewarded. Refuse, and you will spend your life toiling in manual labor, and your pain will feed me and my people."

After calming Javer and Brall, my beast has awoken, and he roars in protest at being forced to hide for so very long. I tighten the chains I keep wrapped around him. I haven't let him out since the Fae magic trapped us here. Dragon shifters—any shifters, really—carry so much magic within us that if the King knew, he would find a way to imprison me and torture me for an eternity.

But every time I'm close to Aurelia, my dragon fights even harder to escape. He knows she belongs to us. She's our mate. White hot flames lick along my spine, and I run from the square. I don't stop until I'm deep into the tall trees that surround this place. Here, no one will see me. Or the fire I need to release before my dragon takes over.

Closing my eyes, I clench my fists and take a deep breath. As I release it, a stream of fire hits the mossy undergrowth. It rained two nights ago, and the flames don't catch, only fizzle out in the damp foliage.

"You will *not* take control," I manage as the monster inside me fights to be freed. "If I let you out, we both die."

The beast whines, but deep down, I know he understands. And now, some of his frustration released, I can go back to the market. Today, *I* will purchase one of Aurelia's blankets. And if she lets me, perhaps I'll finally be able to kiss her.

CHAPTER TWO

AURELIA

The crowds part as the King and the Prince walk through the market, followed by four Fae guards. They are all beautiful in an odd sort of way. Blond, nearly white hair, perfect skin. But I can see through the facade. Their eyes, so pale they are almost silver, give them away.

Disdain. Disgust. A desperate need for power. That is what I see. They feed off of the suffering of others, and if they are in the wrong mood, they purposely torment the outcasts, threatening us with imprisonment or death.

Those of us with useful skills can often escape scrutiny. But not always.

"What do you have for me today?" the King asks as he and his entourage stop in front of my tent.

"My liege," I say with a little curtsey. "The finest yearling wool cloak, hand-dyed and tightly woven." Spreading the dark blue garment over my table, I wait for the King and the Prince to examine it.

Neither look pleased, so I duck down and withdraw the most perfect, beautiful garments I have ever crafted.

"I also have these." The silk tunics have taken me over a year. So many late nights, spinning and weaving until my fingers were raw and almost bleeding. One is embellished with dark red accents, and the other, a rich green. "I-I made one for each of you."

Fear churns in my belly, and the Prince inhales deeply. "What is your name, spinner?"

"Aurelia, my liege." My voice falters, and I lower my gaze.

"These are passable, Lia," the Prince says, his tone full of disdain.

Passable? They are my best work!

"Watch yourself," the King says sharply, and I gasp. It has long been rumored that the Fae can read our thoughts and our deepest desires, but until now, I did not believe such things. "We will take them, spinner. The cloak as well."

As they head for the next booth—without paying, of course —I stagger back and sink to my knees. I want to vomit, but I cannot let them see how frightened I am. It would only antagonize them further.

Roarke rushes over to me, ducking into the back of my tent and helping me to my feet. "Breathe, darling," he whispers in my ear.

"You cannot be here." I struggle from his hold, but I am too unsteady, and I lean into him, relishing the strong muscles, how warm he is, and his protective embrace. "They will see."

"Let them. I give them enough magic to earn the occasional...indulgence." He spits out the words, his anger pulsing with each beat of his heart against my back.

"My apologies for running off before," he says. "After breaking up the fight, I thought it best to let my head clear."

"You owe me no explanation." Despite enjoying his closeness, the way his spicy, rich scent envelopes me, I should not allow myself to be distracted. I still have five blankets, two shawls, and a dozen pairs of socks left to sell, and while we are so far north that the sun this time of year is near constant, the market could end at any time. The King and the Prince have been known to ring the bell to stop all sales on a whim.

They have moved on, now three stalls away, and I find the strength to extricate myself from Roarke's hold.

Digging his hand into his pocket, Roarke comes away with five silver coins and presses them into my hand. "I will take this beautiful specimen," he says as he nods at my most expensive blanket—a deep purple with white snow-capped mountains along the lower edge. It's the largest in my collection, and I worked for months on it.

"Roarke—" I'm well aware of how he finds an outcast each market day and plies them with coins on the condition they purchase something from me, and I cannot allow him to continue this foolish pursuit.

"Do not argue, my darling," he murmurs as he runs his hand over the blanket, then folds it twice and tucks it under his arm. "The snows will be here before we know it, and this will ensure I do not freeze while I am *alone* in my cottage."

"I find it hard to believe you are ever alone. Unless it is by choice," I tease. Roarke is, by far, the most desirable man in this realm, and both outcasts and wealthy alike vie for his attentions. I do not know why he continues to waste his time with me.

With a quick glance at the Fae, he leans in. "I want only you, Aurelia. One day, you will agree to be mine." Taking my hand, he brushes a kiss to my knuckles, and then strides off with the blanket, leaving me speechless.

~

WITH ONLY A FEW of my wares left, I smile at every passerby, hoping to tempt one or two more. Until an angry, slurred voice breaks through the din of the crowd. "My credit has always been sufficient before!"

I cringe as my father snatches a basket of eggs away from another outcast—a chicken-tender named Giselle. He stumbles, and one of the precious brown globes falls to the ground and shatters.

Giselle calls for aid, and by the time I make it out of my tent, my father has attracted the attention of not only the Fae guards, but the King and Prince as well.

"You will stop this nonsense immediately," the King orders in a thundering voice. "On your knees, human. Or you will spend time in the dungeons."

An egg flies across the aisle and hits the King in the chest. The yolk stains the white stripe down the side of his black tunic, and he stares at my father with pure rage in his eyes.

"You keep us trapped here," my father spits as he throws another egg. "Most of us can barely feed our families. We work day and night, and *you* reap the benefits—feeding off of our misery, of our pain. And then you *grace* us with your presence on Market days and expect us to bow down to you?" A third egg smacks the Prince in the cheek, and the King's guards grab my father's arms and pin them behind his back.

"That has earned you a death sentence," the King roars.

"No! Stop!" I skid to a halt in front of the King and the Prince. They're both impossibly tall, and without a table of goods between us, they seem so much more imposing.

Falling to my knees, I clasp my hands in front of me. "Do not kill him, please. He is all I have left in this world."

"You are the spinner," the King says. His son leans closer to him and whispers in his ear. "Ah. Lia, is it?"

The nickname grates along my spine, but I keep my voice neutral. "Aurelia, my liege. My father has had too much to drink, and he knows not what he says or does. I will take him home and ensure this does not happen again. I have several blankets left and I offer them all to you."

"Silence!" With a wave of his hand, the King steals the air from my lungs. I choke, my fingers clawing at my chest and my throat until my vision starts to darken. Just before I fear I'll pass out, he snaps his fingers, and I can breathe again. "Stand, woman."

I scramble to my feet, though I'm dizzy, and when I throw my hands out to try to stabilize myself, it's the Prince who takes hold of me. "Lia would make an acceptable mate, Father."

A mate? I shake my head, certain I must have misheard, but the King grins, a perfectly straight, blindingly white smile. "You wish her for your own?"

"I do."

"You will have to win her."

My anger flares, and I struggle, but the Prince's grip is too tight. "I am not a prize."

The King's eyes narrow, and he grabs my chin hard enough I fear he'll leave bruises. "That is exactly what you will be unless you wish your father to die this night."

"Aurelia," Father cries as the guards shove him to the ground. One places a booted foot on the back of his neck. "Give him what he wants."

Tears burn my eyes. How can he say such a thing? I begged

for mercy, and my father is willing to simply trade my life for his?

"Do you care for me so little?" I ask in a small voice.

"No. But I have nothing to offer them but you." He starts to cry. Both the King's and the Prince's eyes widen as they draw power from his suffering, before they turn to me.

"I will spare your pitiful father's life," the King says, tightening his grip on my jaw to the point I whimper in pain. "Provided you agree to a bargain. Otherwise, I will simply kill you both."

Both of us?

"Yes. Both of you. My patience has been tried too much this day, and it has been some time since we held a public execution. The energy from such an event..." The King shudders with sick pleasure. "It is so very plentiful."

"What are your terms?" I whisper. All around us, the townspeople have gathered, and yet none of them say a word. I search the crowd for Roarke, and I find him just over the Prince's right shoulder with two other magic bearers holding him back as he tries to get to me. His hazel eyes practically glow, and his hands are balled into fists at his sides. Silently, I beg him for help, but I know he cannot come to my aid. The Fae are more powerful than all of us, and his friends are doing what they must to ensure he does not also die.

Releasing my chin, the King rubs his hands together. "You will be taken to the castle and put to work for my court. We could use a spinner of our own. If you refuse to perform your assigned duties, you will be punished, but otherwise, *I* will not harm you."

"For how long?"

"That," the King says, "is up to you." He glances at his son. "Three nights and days should suffice at a minimum. However, I anticipate it will be much longer."

"Three days' work for my father's life? And mine? There must be some sort of catch."

"Oh, there is, my dear." His lips pull into a grin, and inclines his head towards the Prince.

"And what might that be?" Fear tightens in my chest, and the feel of the Prince's hands on my arms makes my skin crawl.

"For the entirety of your time with us, my son will court you. He will be able to use all of the powers of our kind—and they are many—to win your love. To be released, you must say his name and declare that you are not in love with him. Otherwise, on the night of the second full moon that passes with you as our guest, you will wed him and be bound to him forever."

"Aurelia, do not agree to this."

The hissing words seem to float on the air and wrap themselves around me like a cloak. My gaze finds Roarke again, and somehow, I know...they're his words. But how? No one else seems to hear them. He is not Fae. I would know. And even the Fae cannot do this.

"I will never fall in love with a Fae," I vow and try to shake off the Prince's grip, but he holds fast.

"Give us your answer, Lia," the Prince demands as he spins me around to face him. His silvery eyes mesmerize me, and even with Roarke's voice in the back of my mind, I have no choice. I have to do this or my father and I will both die.

"I agree to your terms."

CHAPTER THREE

ROARKE

*N*o!

At my sides, two other magic-bearers, Valinor and Crux, struggle to hold me back.

"Watch yourself, Roarke," Valinor hisses in my ear. "You cannot best the King. Not with four guards protecting him."

Crux mutters quietly, "His obsession with that outcast will get him killed one day."

When I growl and meet his gaze, Crux falls silent. Smart. My dragon is so close to the surface, I fear I will lose control. "If you *ever* refer to her as 'less than' again, I will personally rip out your heart and feed it to you."

The warlock seems to deflate before my eyes, but he does not release his hold on me. The spelled ground siphons our magic, and if we are not careful, the King will sense us. I suspect Valinor is a werewolf and has been hiding that fact for decades.

Aurelia stands perfectly still, caught in the Prince's thrall.

Damn Fae and their ability to compel their human victims. The King summons a long black rope with a snap of his fingers, then gestures to Aurelia. Wordlessly, she presents her hands, wrists crossed, and the rope wraps around them so tightly, pain flits across her beautiful features.

Another length of rope winds around her torso, effectively binding her arms to her slender frame from shoulders to elbows.

Still, she barely flinches until the Prince pulls a handkerchief from his pocket and blindfolds her. Aurelia's chest heaves, and I can scent her fear even from across the square. The end of the rope dangles from her bound wrists, and the King uses it as a leash, gripping it tightly and yanking her forward, hard.

She stumbles and crashes into his chest, but he shoves her towards his son who catches her and strokes his hands down her sides, all the way to her hips.

My dragon rails against his confinement, and if he were a physical being, he'd claw through my chest in his rage. I cannot watch the woman I hoped would one day be my mate suffer like this, but if I attack now, I am assuring my death as well as hers.

"Let. Me. Go," I say. "I will not attack them. But I cannot let her out of my sight. Not until I must."

Whatever Crux and Valinor hear in my voice assures them if they do not do as I ask, they will die, and they release my arms, but Valinor steps in front of me before I can follow Aurelia.

"We have survived this long because we do not make trouble, Roarke. This may be a pitiful existence compared to what we once knew, but we *are* still alive. See that you stay that way."

I nod, clapping him on the shoulder as I duck around him to the edge of the square.

The King leads Aurelia away, the Prince as his side, and I skirt the realm's tavern and hide in an alley, pressing my forehead to the cool stone wall.

Bide your time. She is guaranteed to live for the next three days. The Fae do not lie. Tonight, you can try to find a way into the tower and rescue her.

I do not know what I will possibly do after that. They will come for us. But I cannot let her suffer there alone.

They're coming closer. To reach the tower, they will pass my hiding spot, and I sink further into the shadows. "Please," Aurelia begs. "Take off the blindfold. I am not fighting you."

"You belong to us now, and you will obey," the King snarls and jerks the rope again. Aurelia falls to her knees with a whimper, and my dragon roars in my head, desperate to put an end to her tormentors.

The Prince lifts her to her feet, and his smooth voice makes me want to rip out his throat. "There, there, my sweet, Lia. You will soon come to trust us. We know best. *I* know best."

"Never," she hisses.

"You say that now. But once you are within the tower walls, you will understand." He slaps her ass, and she yelps.

"Do not touch me!"

"Enough!" The King stops and holds out his hand. "Handkerchief. Now."

One of the guards passes him a strip of cloth, and he gags Aurelia tightly. "I tire of her protests, son. I want her locked as far from my chambers as possible. Humans are so...loud, and this one will scream. I am certain of it."

Fuck me. If the Prince harms one hair on her head, I will find a way to let my dragon eviscerate him. The Fae's only weakness is iron, and they believe they have rid the realm of every last bit of it. But surely...some must remain. This land is ancient, and they stole it a mere two centuries ago. If I can find even a small amount...I can weaken them. Perhaps enough to kill them. With the King dead, the magic that keeps us all prisoner will fall, and I can escape this place with the woman I love.

❧

AURELIA

The ropes make it hard to breathe. They're so tight, and without being able to see, I take short, quick steps, terrified with every one that I'll fall again. That the Prince will put his hands on me. That he won't be satisfied with a quick grope, and will touch me in places no man has ever been.

The dirt turns hard under my boots, and the warmth of the sun fades. This time of year, the nights last only an hour or two, so it can't be dark on the other side of the blindfold, but wherever we are, the sun does not wish to be.

The corners of my mouth ache from the rough fabric gagging me, and my hands are numb. Three days. I can resist for three days. There is nothing the King or the Prince could possibly to do to me to persuade me to marry that bastard in so short a time. They will force me to work. But he swore he would not harm me.

The King utters words in a language I do not understand, and the sounds of stones scraping against one another send a shiver down my spine. We're at the castle, and though I have no choice, I pull against the ropes, desperately trying to get away—but bound, gagged, and blindfolded, there's nowhere I could possibly run.

A snap of fingers is quickly followed by the Prince throwing me over his shoulder like a sack of grain. My hands are pinned under me. I flail my legs, hoping to catch him in a delicate spot, but he clamps a second arm around my calves and holds them tightly to his chest.

The bouncing as he climbs set after set of stairs makes me want to vomit, but I swallow the urge and try to count. At least twenty floors. We must be close to the top of one of the towers.

Metal. A heavy lock. The creak of wood. And then I'm back on my feet, pushed against something hard and thin that runs vertically down to my feet. A beam, perhaps? More ropes wrap around me, binding me to the beam all the way down to my knees. I cannot move, and I scream through the cloth between my teeth.

"This is your new home, my sweet Lia," the Prince says, his voice dripping with fake concern. "I do hope you enjoy your time here." His lips brush my parted ones, and I'd recoil if I had anywhere to go.

He would not leave me here, would he? Bound and gagged, unable to move or lie down? All night?

Footsteps recede, the door slams and locks, and I start to cry. Yes. That is exactly what he intends to do.

CHAPTER FOUR

AURELIA

Time means nothing trapped in a perpetual haze of pain and fear. My only indication it passes at all is the hunger and thirst building inside me, the weakness of my limbs, and the pounding in my head.

The ropes cut into the skin of my wrists, my tongue is bone dry, and I'm bound so thoroughly, I can't even sink down to the floor to rest my aching feet. More than once, I've fallen asleep for a moment or two, then woken to the agony of my entire body bucking against the restraints.

The worst, though, is the silence. It makes me grateful for the pain, because it proves I still live. I do not know what I believed would happen when I stepped inside these stone walls, but it was not this.

With nothing but my thoughts to distract me from the unending fear I will die before anyone comes back for me, I try to recall happier times. My grandmother's kindly face, the way

I'd sit at her feet and play with my simple straw doll as she told stories.

"Your grandfather was whip smart," she says as she brushes my hair. "He found scraps and shavings of iron scattered through the realm, and he collected them. He was determined to forge a weapon —just in case he ever found a way to kill the King. Your mother was but a young thing. Only eighteen when he'd collected enough iron to make a single blade. He intended to put an end to the Fae's control of us and free the entire realm."

I stare up at her, wide-eyed and confused. "But we are not free."

She sighs, and her eyes turn sad. "He convinced fifty of the realm's strongest men to join him, and many more pledged their support, though they were hesitant. On Market day, the fifty of them surrounded the Fae King and his guards. Your grandfather was quick, and he stabbed one of the guards with the iron blade, then tried to kill the King. But a second guard jumped in front of the King at the last moment.

"He started a war—the only war we have ever fought with the Fae. But it lasted less than two days. The King and his court used their magic to ruin the lands. The sheep started to die, the crops withered, and darkness blanketed the realm. They poisoned the water, and by the second morning, more than a hundred were dead, and all fifty of the men who'd participated in the attack surrendered themselves to the King. That was the last I ever saw of your grandfather."

I force my head up, the only part of my body I can control, and try to stretch my neck. It does little good. My father is safe. For now. The King promised he would remain free, and though the Fae are evil tricksters, they cannot lie. That is my only comfort.

Some time later, the door opens with a loud *thunk*, and I jerk in my bonds. Terror sends my heart racing, my breaths tearing from my chest in short, frantic pants.

"You poor thing." The Prince's smooth voice is right next to my ear, so close I whimper weakly as my instincts kick in and I try to pull my head away. But he grabs a fistful of my hair. "Stay still, my bride, and I will ease some of your discomfort."

Not your bride.

He loosens the gag, ripping it from my mouth and sending the worst pain I have ever felt along my tongue and the corners of my lips where the fabric had stuck. I scream, and he covers my mouth. "You must learn to behave, or I will silence you another way. Perhaps one much more permanent."

Sobbing, I nod, and he removes his hand. At this point, I'll do anything he wants if he'll just untie me, and I am about to tell him so when the ropes fall away, so quickly it must be by magic, and I collapse into his arms.

My body holds no strength, and he carries me a few steps, then sits with me in his lap. I can feel his erection pressing into my bottom, and I want to shove at him, but I cannot move.

Something presses to my lips, and then the sweetest taste fills my mouth. My grandmother's warning echoes through my mind a moment too late.

"Do not accept food or drink from the Fae's hand. Their magic will consume you, and you will never want to leave them."

I swallow on instinct, my hunger and thirst in this moment overwhelming, and the Prince croons to me in his native tongue, words I don't understand but that I know, deep down, are meant to sway me, to bind me to him in a way I cannot allow.

Still, I do not resist, and my body floats as I drink my fill. I'm only dimly aware of him laying me down and brushing his lips to my cheek. "You will come to love it here, my sweet Lia. And you will love me. I know it."

I still can't see. He never removed the blindfold, but even if he had, I lack the strength to open my eyes. Sleep pulls me under, and in my dreams, he comes to me, comforts me, and I want to give in, but then a deep voice—one I recognize but cannot place—sends warmth all through me.

Fight him, Aurelia. I will come for you. Even if I must die, I will save you.

~

THE PRINCE

My beauty rests, the sweet draught I gave her too powerful for any being to fight. Blindfolded, helpless, lashed to the post in the center of this barren room, she was perfection when I entered. Her pain strengthens me, feeds my power, and the more I make her suffer, the more she will desire me.

"Come," I command, and two of the King's guards enter the room. One carries a spinning wheel, and the other balances a bale of straw across his shoulders. My father's plan is brilliant. Give her an impossible task, punish her severely when she fails, and then offer her another bargain. One she will be too weak to refuse.

My father claimed my mother in a similar fashion, though my methods will be slightly more...severe. After all, this human woman was strong enough to offer herself in sacrifice to save that pitiful drunkard, Abbot. She will not sway to my side easily.

"Pile the straw three bales high along that wall," I say, and the guards nod, leaving the room to retrieve the rest of what I am certain will become the thing my future bride hates most in this world.

When nine bales line one side of the tower room, I dismiss them, taking a final moment to watch her sleep. Already I can sense her emotions. Her fear of me abates with the draught and my magic, and something akin to gratefulness replaces it.

After all, it was the King who bound her. I released her. Saved her. And tomorrow...I will begin wooing her.

❦

"Did you see to your new pet?" the King asks as I join him in his favorite sitting room.

I sink down onto thick cushions and accept the whiskey one of the servants hands me. "I did. She drank from my cup, and the room is ready for her. She will fail your task, and when I offer her a second bargain, she will have no choice but to agree."

"Noelle!" My father's booming voice fills the room, and a moment later, the woman who birthed me rushes in. She is not my mother. Not truly. I did not even meet her until I had passed into adulthood.

"Yes, my King?" She keeps her eyes downcast, her hands clasped in front of her. Even at the human age of two hundred twenty and four, she looks only slightly older than my soon-to-be-bride. Thanks to my father's magic.

"Sit."

She hesitates for only a moment before taking her place on his lap, and I roll my eyes at the obvious display of power. His fingers dig into her hip, and she stifles a wince. "My precious, we have a new guest in the tower room. She is to be our son's bride."

Noelle turns her head and glares at my father. "You swore to me you would never take another by force—"

"I did no such thing." He squeezes her tighter, and she makes a sharp, pained noise. "The girl traded her freedom for

23

the life of her worthless father. I offered her a bargain, and she took it. You understand how that works."

"How could you?" she whispers and swipes a tear from her cheek. "She will never leave this place, and her life will be nothing but misery and pain."

"Like yours, I suppose?" Father shoves her off his lap and onto the floor. "You will live centuries because of what I give you. You have the finest clothing, the richest wine, and the softest bed in the realm."

"You took my sons!" she cries. "You locked Adrian in chains and minutes after he was born, you had your guards take Rumpel—"

My father backhands her, sending her tumbling, and she starts to sob. "I took the boy from you to save him, so he would not end up like his worthless brother," the King growls. "And I offered you a bargain in exchange. You would live to see him grown, have everything you wish for—save freedom—and be revered by all who make their home in this castle. And you would retain the use of your tongue. Provided you never spoke his name again."

Her eyes go wide, and she clamps her hands over her mouth.

"You have violated our bargain, and so you will suffer the consequences." He hauls her up by her wrist and drags her from the room as I finish my drink and pour myself another.

The pleading look she gives me as he takes her away should affect me. But instead, her fear gives me a burst of power, and I relish in it. I am a trickster, immortal, and above all—my father's favorite son.

My brother will never see freedom again, all because I had father's ear and Noelle corrupted Adrian with useless *human* emotions. If Father had let her raise me, I am certain I would be as useless as Adrian. Thankfully, Father forbade her from even seeing me until I was grown, not wanting me to suffer the pitiful trappings of empathy and love.

And I am stronger for it.

CHAPTER FIVE

Darkness is finally close, though it is well past midnight. This time of year, the night rules for mere hours, and the sun bathes the realm in warmth long past the time most settle in to sleep and long before they wake.

I cannot to go to Aurelia in the castle tonight as much as I want to. I need information, time to plan, and rest. But I will not return to my cottage until I speak to the idiot who condemned her to three days in hell—with an option on eternity.

My knock goes unanswered. So I pound harder. The shuffling sound of drunken footsteps angers me, and I huff out a breath that escapes in a puff of steam. My beast wants Abbott to pay for ever putting Aurelia in this position. The man does as well, but he knows there is a time for violence and a time for understanding, and I must resist beating the man to a bloody pulp or burning him alive. For now.

Though I am not ruling out the eventuality.

"Who're you?" Aurelia's father slurs as he leans against the door jamb.

"The man who wanted to claim your daughter as his mate and protect her forever. Until *your* stupidity put her life in peril." I push past him and enter my love's home. It smells of her. Of wool and dye and lavender. And the town's cheapest beer.

Abbot trudges after me, his shoulders slumped and his gait uneven. "She is gone. The Prince will never release her."

"He will. If only because I will remove his head. But I need information before I try to breach the castle. I do not have run-ins with the Prince. The Fae do not bother those of us with... certain abilities."

Sinking down onto an old, rickety chair, Abbot squints up at me. "What abilities?"

"Are you that daft? I am a magic bearer. As long as I feed some of my power into the ley lines that traverse this realm, lines the Fae tap into whenever they wish, they leave me be. You never knew this?" Frowning, I search the small room for a suitable place to sit. There isn't one. Not really. A rickety table with three chairs, a threadbare sofa that clearly doubles as Aurelia's bed, and the floor.

Needing to be close to her, desperate to have her scent wrapped around me, I lower myself carefully onto the sofa. The blanket neatly folded along the back is her work, and I take it reverently into my hands and inhale deeply. "What *do* you know of this realm? When did you come here?"

"I was twenty," he says as he drops his head into his hands. "I never asked any questions once I found out I couldn't leave. I tried. For so many days. Until Aurelia's mother found me in the forest, half-dead, and brought me back here."

Aurelia's mother. Not my wife or my mate.

His words hold so much shame. Is this the reason he has been a drunkard for as long as I can remember?

"Aurelia is not your daughter."

The man starts to sob, his shoulders shaking. "No. June was already pregnant when she found me. Not far along. We told everyone the baby had come early."

My beast is quiet now, listening intently as I ask my next question."Who is her father?"

Abbot pulls a handkerchief from his pocket and blows his nose loudly before swiping at his reddened, puffy cheeks. "One of the King's guards. He was killed when June's father attacked him for defiling his daughter."

Aurelia is half Fae.

Inside me, the dragon rails, his sorrow and horror so great, my own eyes burn. If the Prince or the King were ever to learn of her true heritage, they would never let her go—no matter what bargains were made. They would consider her half forfeit and keep her forever.

Anger pulses through my every nerve, and I spring for the dolt in front of me, haul him to his feet, and slam him against the wall hard enough he hiccups.

The stench of alcohol is overwhelming.

"Listen carefully, and perhaps, you will live to see her again," I snarl. He looks up at me, his eyes wide and most definitely sober. Now. "If you *ever* tell another soul of her parentage, I will rip out your spine and make you watch as I shatter each bone. I have enough magic within me to keep you alive—and screaming—until I am done. Do you understand?"

"Y-yes," he stammers. "I...I killed her, didn't I? The Prince will kill her, and it will be all my fault."

"That is still to be determined. Now tell me. Do you have *any* iron in this house? Even a single scrap. A shaving. *Anything.*"

Abbot nods, and hope flares to life, soothing my raging dragon and giving me a few blessed moments of peace.

"Get it. Whatever you have. Right. Now." Releasing my grip, I start to pace as he shuffles off into the bedroom I assume he once shared with Aurelia's mother. I remember her now. Beautiful, but always sad. And I wonder...was it because she loved the Fae guard who gave her his seed? Or because she hated him?

A few moments later, Abbot returns with something wrapped in cloth cradled in his hands. "This belonged to Aurelia's grandfather. He...right after I came, there was a war. It... wasn't what everyone thinks. Not really."

I stagger back as the pieces fall into place. "Do you mean to tell me that the man who started the two-day war, who nearly caused the death of every last being in this realm without Fae blood in their veins, did so—"

"Because he wanted to kill the Fae guard who'd taken his daughter's virtue." Abbot nods and passes me the object.

This...if this is what I think it is, I have just found all I need to murder both the King and the Prince and reclaim Aurelia's freedom. I pull the leather tie loose and unfold the rough muslin. The dagger inside is covered with a thin layer of rust, but I do not care. Rust means iron and iron means death to those who would keep her from me.

Quickly, I wrap the weapon up again and tuck it inside my coat pocket. "I do not trust you. Not with how you fancy the drink. Until I free Aurelia, you will be the *guest* of one of my acquaintances. You will not be harmed, but nor will you be able to do any further damage."

"I'll do anything you ask," he says softly. "I don't even care if you kill me, Roarke. Just get Aurelia out of there."

"For her sake, you will live. If it were up to me?" I pat my pocket. "This would be the end of you."

THE REALM IS LARGE, and more than twenty kilometers separate Crux's cottage from Abbot's hovel. But the beast inside me enhances my speed, and I carry Abbot slung over my shoulder. When I told him we would be using magic to travel, he begged me to knock him out, which I did. With a solid punch to the jaw. Happily.

"Roarke?" Crux says as he opens the door and stares at the unconscious man.

"I require a favor. Bind this idiot with your magic and keep him hidden—and silent—until I return." Striding into Crux's main room, I arch a brow. "Where would you like him?"

The warlock mutters something he should likely not repeat in my presence, then sighs. "In the basement." He leads me into his kitchen, then slides his wood stove along the wall to reveal a trap door. No human would be strong enough to move that stove alone, but with the aid of magic...

"You are certain the Fae do not know of this place?" I ask as I lay Abbot on a pallet of blankets.

"What do you take me for, Roarke? A complete dumbass? I may have only been in this realm for thirty years, but I am well aware of how things work." Crux moves around the small space, lighting candles with his magic.

Kneeling, I slap Abbot's cheek. "Wake. Now."

He groans and opens his eyes. "I hate magic."

"Well, I detest humans, and your host is a warlock, so you might want to watch your words."

Abbot focuses on Crux, a healthy amount of fear in his eyes. The warlock offers him an evil smile and points to the corner. "Chamber pot there. Water in a jug on that back table, and cured lamb meat in the cabinet. Make any noise at all, try to escape, and I will truss you up like a Christmas goose."

"I won't," Abbot says as he scoots back on the blankets.

"Keep him here until I return," I say. "If for any reason, I am not back in seven days…" I stop on the stairs with a shake of my head. "Well, then I am dead, and you may do with him what you will."

Crux grabs my arm. "If you don't return, he'll regret the day he was born."

As I shake him off and continue up the stairs, Abbot murmurs, "I already do."

CHAPTER SIX

Awareness returns slowly. In bits and pieces. First, scents. Straw and damp stone. Then, utter and complete silence. I remember the silence.

Fear winds its way through my body as I open my eyes to total darkness. But I also feel the cloth tied tightly around my head.

He never removed the blindfold.

The fear turns to panic, and I suck in sharp breaths as I sit up.

I can move my arms. He untied me.

Lifting my hands to my face, I pull off the rough fabric, then squeeze my eyes closed as the harsh morning light blinds me.

Light. There's a window. A window means there's a chance I can escape. Until I remember how many flights of stairs we climbed. And how weak I was when the Prince released me from my bonds. I don't even know if I can walk, let alone find a way down from any sort of height.

Bringing my hand up to shield my eyes, I risk opening them to slits. The pain is less now, and the room starts to come into focus.

A spinning wheel rests in the very center, and beyond that...bales of straw. My head pounds, and when I try to stand, the room pitches and I crumple to the floor with a whimper.

And then the Prince is at my side. Was he watching me the whole time?

"You are still feeling the after-effects of my father's compulsion," he says softly. His hands are gentle, gathering me close, pressing a cup to my lips. "Drink, Lia. This will help."

My name is not Lia.

Despite his use of a name I hate, I comply immediately. The cool, sweet liquid tastes like heaven, and after a few sips, I feel strong enough to hold the cup on my own, but the Prince bats my hands away.

"No. You will let me help you."

My arms fall, my hands landing in my lap, and I give in, though I know I should not.

"Good girl. Finish it now, Lia. You will feel much better soon. I have your morning meal as well."

Food. I would give anything for food. My stomach growls, and the Prince chuckles. "I am so very sorry you had to go hungry for so long. The cooks were all asleep when we arrived last night. But you will never want for anything again. Not as long as you are in my care."

My eyes flutter closed as I rest my head on his shoulder. He shifts me slightly, and the most delicious smells waft over me.

"Keep your eyes closed, my sweet," he says, and I obey without a second thought. I'm warm, held, and about to eat. What more could I want? Something touches my lips, and I open for him, moaning as what I think is salted pork hits my tongue. Next, a bite of fluffy, honeyed cake, dredged in syrup, then, another sip of nectar.

By the time I hear the scrape of a plate along the wooden floor, my belly is full, and all I want to do is stay in this moment forever. Except, I'm forgetting something. I'm supposed to...fight? Fight who?

"Do you want me, Lia?" the Prince asks. "We could be so happy together. Accept me now, and you will have every comfort."

"I...n-no?" My thoughts are so muddled they do not feel like my own, and I try to force my eyes open, but my lids are so heavy, I cannot seem to make them move.

The Prince's arm tightens around my shoulders, and he presses his hand over my heart "You want me. You need me. You love me."

A shudder racks my entire body, like a piece of me is waking up after so long asleep. But then, there's warmth and the brush of lips to my cheek, and the gesture is so tender, tears prick my eyes.

"I...want..." The urge to say yes, to beg this man to keep me safe is strong, but he is not who I am supposed to be with. His touch feels...wrong. Almost painful.

Memories assault my mind. Ropes winding around my body. Being unable to breathe. Falling, my wrists bound, the King's laugh. My father's screams. Pain at the corners of my mouth. Gagged. Tied to a beam. Left until I was too weak to move.

And Roarke. His scent. His fingers stroking mine. His laugh.

"No!" I shove my hands against the Prince's chest as I force my eyes open. His face is twisted in anger, and though I manage to scoot back a short distance, it isn't enough. He strikes me across the cheek, and I yelp. "You...spelled me!"

And I will do so every fucking day until you give in.

His lips do not move, but I hear his enraged voice in my head as clearly as if he had spoken. His expression shifts, morphing into one of stern disapproval mixed with...a decidedly patronizing look. "I did no such thing, Lia. I cared for you. Like I will care for you every day for the rest of your life."

"And would you hit me every day as well?" Wrapping my arms tightly around my body, I find the bruises from so long bound, and I use the pain in my ribs, along with the throbbing in my jaw, to help me focus. "You do not care for me. You only want to control me." I must get out of here. My gaze flies to the door over his shoulder, and hope fades with the sight of the two very large, very angry looking Fae guards blocking any escape.

The Prince roars an oath and wraps his fingers around my wrist as he jumps up. The motion sends a shock of pain through my shoulder as he drags me across the room, then hauls me to my feet.

Fresh air drifts over my cheeks, but as I focus on the window, I want to cry.

"Look," he snarls as he presses his body to mine. I must have miscounted the previous night. We aren't twenty floors up. It is at least thirty. The people on the ground look so small, and the tower is as smooth as a blade of grass. Nothing to hold onto, no ledges, no outcroppings. If I try to escape through this window, I will die.

He pushes me forward, bending me over the sil so my upper body is hanging beyond the boundaries of the stone. I cannot breathe. My throat seizes, and my lungs spasm as I desperately struggle for air. It is as if a chain has tightened around my chest, and panic consumes me. My arms and legs flail helplessly.

"Do you feel that, my future bride?" he sneers. "That is the power of the bargain you made with the Fae. Until you can say my name and tell me you do not want me, my father's air magic will stop you from venturing one foot outside the tower walls. You will stay here or you will *die*."

As my vision narrows, pinpricks of light and dark vying for dominance, the Prince grabs a thick chunk of my hair, pulls me upright, and then sends me reeling across the room where I crash into the cot I woke on.

Hoarse, wheezing breaths escape my chest as the magic relinquishes its hold on me, and I glare up at him. "I...do not... want you...*Braxton*."

That should be it. I should be free. But the Prince only laughs. At first, it is merely a scoff, but then, the sound turns to a deep, all-consuming chortle as he braces his hands on his knees. "You foolish human. Braxton is the name we let slip from time to time, just to trap humans like you. A Fae's true name is their most closely guarded secret. You belong to *me* now, Lia. Because you will never know me as anything other than your master and your mate."

"My name is Aurelia." The words escape weaker than I intend, his admission shaking me to my very core.

"Your name," he snaps as he towers over me with his hands on his hips, "is whatever I wish it to be. You should be thankful I do not choose a different one. Like whore. Harlot. *Slave*."

I cower in the face of his rage. "You wouldn't..."

"Do not test me." He points to the spindle, then sweeps his arm out to gesture to the bales of straw against the wall. "The King has decreed that your assigned duty is to spin this straw into gold. If you cannot, per the terms of our bargain, you will be punished. And he has left your punishment up to me. Two days bound to the beam should suffice, I think. You have until tomorrow morning."

"You said you would not hurt me," I say as I try—and fail—

to get to my feet. The room spins, and I fall back on my bottom once more.

"You need to pay better attention, harlot. My *father* said he would hot harm you. I made no such promise."

Before I can protest, he stalks out of the room, and the door slams shut, a heavy lock clanging in his wake.

The Fae have won. My tears tumble freely as I huddle in my solitary prison. I have no food, no water—only a chamber pot and a window I cannot even stick my head out of. And I am to spin straw into gold. I could not spin *gold* into gold, let alone straw.

My gaze lands on the beam in the center of the room. Two days. There is no way I can survive two days without breaking. Without giving in to the Prince's charms. I know now...he did not leave me there all night. At most, it was four or five hours.

Two days and I will give him whatever he asks for.

The stone floor is hard under my bruised and battered body, and I do the only thing I can. Crawl onto the cot, burrow under the lone blanket, and sob until I have no more tears left to cry.

CHAPTER SEVEN

ROARKE

I cannot sleep for more than a few hours at a time. My worry for Aurelia grows stronger with each breath I take, and after a day of pacing and planning, I turn the dagger over and over in my hands.

The rust is gone now, but I have the dust saved in a small pouch I tuck into my pocket. I will not waste a single speck of this precious metal that may be our only hope.

Crux reports that Abbot has not made a sound, thank the gods, and well after the town has started to settle down for the night, I use the forest as cover and head for the Fae castle.

My dragon snarls to be freed, and I soothe him with the promise he will get to spread his wings very soon. There is no way to climb the tower, but with the supplies I have in my pockets, I may be able to rappel down. Windows spaced every five to ten floors offer glimpses inside the structure, and I am certain they will not be keeping her anywhere she could escape easily.

The top floors are my safest bet.

At the very edge of the tree line, I shed my clothing and fold it into a neat pile before securing it with a thick cord of leather. The dagger is within easy reach, its handle protruding slightly from the bundle.

I take a deep breath and release the strict hold I keep on the dragon inside me. His roar fills my ears, but he knows better than to allow anyone but me to hear him.

The bones all along my spine crack and lengthen, and a leathery hide starts to spread along my ribs. My legs, well-muscled as a man, are three times as thick as my entire human body now. Ridges form on my back, and my ears flatten, my eyes grow and elongate, and my teeth transform into lethal sharpened weapons without a second thought.

Swishing his tail, the beast takes over. He grips the leather between his talons and flaps the wings that sprouted from my shoulder blades. He's completely silent as he rises into the air, and our combined magic serves to hide us from view. In flight, we can remain invisible for short periods of time, and that is all we need to reach the very top of the Fae castle.

Circling twice, my dragon sniffs the air, then extends his forked tongue and tastes it. The Fae's magic is all through this place, but there do not appear to be any wards in place. Only residual detritus from past charms.

Setting down gently on the stone and wood roof, my beast snorts, a plume of smoke escaping his nostrils.

"I know. This was not long enough to sate you, but we have a greater need now. Remember. Our mate is here."

He snorts again, but I know he will give in. My physical strength is nothing compared to his, but he lacks the mental control to force me to do anything.

"Can you scent her?"

For the mass he carries, he should shake the entire tower as he moves, but he is graceful to a fault, and almost glides to the edge of the roof before sticking his nose over the side and inhaling deeply.

Moving slowly, checking all directions, he stops halfway around, and the mating call threatens to knock me—and him—on our ass.

Aurelia. Her scent is the strongest here, tinged with salty tears and desperation.

It takes only a handful of moments for the beast to relinquish control back to me, and I rip open my small parcel, don my clothing, and tuck the dagger into the pocket of my coat. The leather strap wraps around one of the tower's capstones, and I lower myself down to the left of her window—or what I hope is her window. If I'm wrong, this could be my last act on this earth.

I creep closer, and when I angle a glance inside, my heart stops beating for a single breath. She's curled on a narrow cot, her face stained with tears and dirt, her blouse torn, and her long black hair mussed. But she is alone.

Pushing off the wall, I twist my body and land in a crouch on the floor inside her room.

"Aurelia," I say quietly as I spring for her.

She jerks, a hoarse scream bubbling up in her throat until I cover her mouth with my hand.

"Shhh, darling. It's Roarke. Do not fight me, please."

After her nod, I release her, and she narrows her swollen and bloodshot eyes at me. "You...cannot be real. This is another trick."

"It is not. I swear it." Her hands are so cold, and I take them in my own. Her wrists bear thick, red welts from the ropes. "I bought a blanket from you yesterday. We almost kissed. And every moment since, I've regretted not being braver.

"Roarke." Aurelia throws her arms around me, and her tears soak into the collar of my shirt.

"I can get you out of here. Come with me." I pick her up and carry her to the window, but her body goes rigid.

"No! You cannot!" She fights to free herself from my hold, but I will not let her stay here, and have one leg over the sil when she chokes and spasms and fists my shirt, pulling hard enough the fabric rips, and I finally take notice of the sheer terror on her face—and the blue cast to her lips.

Once we're back inside, she takes a deep, shuddering breath. "The Fae...charm," she wheezes. "I cannot leave...or I will die."

"What?"

She clings to me, her arms trembling, and her words are too muffled for me to hear as she buries her face against my neck.

"Aurelia, look at me."

She does, terror and shame warring for dominance in her hazel eyes.

"Are any of the Fae likely to come for you in the next few hours? To bring you a meal or..." I leave off *"to torture you."*

"N-no," she whispers. "The Prince said I had until morning to...to do the impossible." Her tears start in earnest once more, and I pull her onto the narrow cot and lean against the wall, Aurelia's back to my chest and my arms around her.

"Take a deep breath, love, and tell me everything."

SHE SPEAKS in hushed tones about her first night, about being too weak, too scared to resist when the Prince fed her charmed food and attempted to trick her into marrying him. My dragon rails when he learns of the King's demand that she spin straw into gold, and how the Prince will punish her when she does not complete the task.

"I will never leave here, Roarke. You should not have come," she says with a sigh, nestling deeper into my embrace.

"You will. If only because I will not accept another conclusion to our story." I press a kiss to the top of her head. "It is your turn to listen now. And to plot your own revenge against the bastards who would harm you so."

"I am helpless here."

"You are not." I shift her into the crook of my arm so I can meet her gaze. "Aurelia, did no one ever tell you the truth of your birth?"

"What do you mean? My mother died when I was born. What more is there to know?" She sniffles and swipes her sleeve across her nose.

This is a risk. One that could end with her rejecting me or the Fae learning the secret she does not even know she keeps.

"Darling, you have seen the sides of the tower. You know there is no way to climb it." I have to know if she will accept me before I tell her the rest.

"How did you—?" she asks.

"I am not human. Nor Fae." Swallowing hard, I take her hands. "I am a dragon. I can transform into a great, winged beast who breathes fire."

Aurelia blinks up at me, then a sound that might be a laugh escapes her swollen lips. Have the Prince's charms addled her mind?

"Aurelia? Did you hear me?"

"Dragons are not real." She shakes her head, a look of pure disbelief on her face. "No. You got in somehow. Snuck into the castle and got to the roof? Then climbed down?"

"I went to the roof, yes. But I flew there." I loosen the buttons on my shirt to reveal a torso covered with scars. Burns

—from playing with my dragon brothers during our childhood —and deep scratches from fighting with werewolves, bears, vampires, and more. "I have been trapped in this realm for decades, Aurelia. Hiding who I am from everyone—especially the Fae."

"This is madness." Aurelia tries to get to her feet, but she wavers, and I catch her before she falls.

"You are ill."

She sags against me and lets me help her back to the cot. "I have not had food nor drink since this morning. And the Prince will ensure I am desperate when he comes to *punish* me."

I kneel in front of her and take her hands. "Aurelia, you must believe me. I *am* a dragon. And you..." I tighten my fingers on hers. "What I am about to say to you must remain secret from the Fae. If it does not...your life will be forfeit."

"Then do not tell me!" Aurelia cries. "I cannot fight him, Roarke. He forces me to drink this sweet nectar from his cup. You know how dangerous it is to accept food and drink from the Fae. After he makes me drink, my mind is no longer my own. I fear...I will tell him everything. I will have no choice. Leave me. *Forget* about me. My life is over. The Prince *will* make me his. But if you go...if you abandon all hope that we can be together—that I can *ever* be free—you might have a chance to survive."

"No, darling. Do not ask this of me." I do the only thing I can think of. I kiss her. Truly kiss her.

She melts in my arms, and I relish the feel of her soft curves. Back on the cot now, I pull her on top of me, sinking my fingers into her hair. I will not let her give up. Not on me, and not on herself.

"Roarke," she whispers as our lips part. "Why must you make me want what I can never have?"

"You can have me. You *will* have me." Carefully cupping her cheek, I brush a tear from the corner of her eye. "I have something for you."

Pulling the bag of iron shavings from my pocket, I press them into her hand. Aurelia shudders. Of course. She is Fae. Can she even wield the dagger? "What is this?" she asks.

"Iron. You can use this against the Prince."

She turns the bag over in her hand as she wriggles off me to sit on the edge of the cot. I miss the feel of her, but our mate bond has already started to form, and hints of her emotions wind their way into my heart. A small spark of hope has taken hold within her.

"How?"

"It will poison him if you can get him to ingest it. But if it comes into contact with his skin, it will weaken him." I nestle her between my thighs and nuzzle the soft skin behind her ear. "I will question every single person in the realm until I find out the Prince's true name."

"What if no one knows?" Aurelia shudders against me.

"Then I will return tonight and we will find a way out of this castle together."

CHAPTER EIGHT

AURELIA

Roarke leaves me at the first light of dawn. He held me for hours, and I actually slept. Comforted. Protected. My eyes are so swollen it is hard to blink, and I have no tears left to cry.

"Take care to hide the bag of shavings, darling," Roarke says as he presses the small bag into my hand once more. I feel sick, knowing he's leaving me, but he cannot stay. If he does, the Fae will find a way to own him too.

My fingers are clumsy, trembling, and Roarke covers them his own, stilling my attempts.

"Remember. This is the Fae's only weakness. Use it if there is no other choice. But hold on for me, Aurelia. I will come for you tomorrow night."

I tuck the bag under the thin mattress before Roarke gathers me in his arms.

"I have loved you since the moment I first saw you," he

says. "You are my mate, and when you are free, I will do much more...than this." His hand slides into my tangled locks, and he angles my head so he can claim my lips.

His kiss makes my knees weak—or perhaps that is the dehydration—but when his tongue teases my lips, I let him in. Something inside me warms, like a flame ignited for the very first time.

"Roarke, please," I moan when I can breathe again.

"Please what?" His erection presses to my stomach, and if I were not trapped under a Fae spell, I would beg him to claim me. To not let the Prince be the one to take my virginity. Because for all Roarke's promises, I know he will fail. The Prince will claim me, and I will be forced to let him.

The tears I thought I could no longer cry start up again, and I wriggle out of his arms. "Please go. If you stay any longer, they will find you. I sealed my own fate trying to save my father. I cannot damn you as well."

"You will not damn me, darling. You are my salvation. Use the iron. If for no other purpose than to make that bastard suffer." Roarke strides for the window, and as he lunges for a long piece of cord I did not notice hanging just to the side of the sil, he glances back at me. "Give me two minutes, Aurelia. Then watch for me and believe. Everything I have told you is the truth. I love you. And I will free you."

And then he pushes off, and the man I should have been free to love is gone.

I cannot help myself. I go to the window.

There is a soft thud, then a sound I do not recognize.

When I see the majestic creature arcing through the sky, I almost forget my curse and stick my head out the window. But before I can do more than lean in, my throat closes, and I take a quick step back. He...Roarke...really is a dragon.

WHEN I LIE BACK DOWN and try to steal another hour or two of sleep, nausea churns in my stomach. I tore into one of the bales of straw, scattering it about the room while I screamed obscenities at the Prince, the King, and even my father. At one point, I even attempted to take some of the straw and separate the fibers as I would with wool. But every time, the straw broke into pieces, leaving me with nothing but bleeding fingers and fear.

I stare at the beam in the center of the room. It runs from the floor all the way to the ceiling. The width of my hand on each side, it will bite into my back until I cannot stand the pain any longer. Skimming my fingers over the welts on my wrists, then my swollen cheek, I shudder. What marks will I bear tomorrow? The next day? And the next?

If I give in... If I agree to marry the Prince, I can save myself this impending agony. But then there's Roarke.

I can still taste him on my lips. If I concentrate, I can separate his scent from the others in the room. My own sweat and tears. The grassy smell of the straw.

Roarke loves me. And by all that is holy in this realm, I love him too. I shouldn't. We are too different. Even if he weren't a dragon, we would still be too different. But I cannot help my heart.

Turning over, I bury my face in the thin mattress—no one bothered to give me a pillow—and fall into a fitful sleep.

"YOU FAILED." The King's voice wakes me, and the shock sends me tumbling to the floor. "There is no gold in this room. My son has suggested two days bound to the beam as punishment."

I scramble back, all the way to the stone wall, and hold up my hands. "Please... No one can spin straw into gold. Give me wool or silk or—"

"Father." The Prince pushes his way into the room and scoops me into his arms. "Leave us. I should be the one to punish my future bride."

"See that you do not fail." The King turns on his heel and strides back through the door, three massive Fae guards parting to let him pass. They form an impenetrable wall once he is gone.

"Put me down," I demand, but he only tightens his hold. "I may be forced to marry you, whatever-your-name-is, but I will *never* want your hands on me."

The Prince does exactly what I ask. He drops me from his full height, and I land on my hip and shoulder. My head slams against the stone floor, and then the Prince starts to speak in that strange language I cannot understand.

My mind clouds, and the pounding behind my eyes builds until I feel as if my head will quite literally split open. Sights and sounds make no sense to me. I see the glint of gold, hear the spinning wheel, and on top of that...a strange tune. A happy song with an air of triumph.

Blinking hard, I try to focus, and when I do, I gasp.

The Prince stands next to the spindle, staring down at me. A spool of golden thread sits on top of one of the bales of straw. "How...?" I push myself up on an elbow, and the room tilts. In two steps, the Prince is kneeling next to me, his hand around my upper arm.

"Fae magic, my sweet Lia." He whispers a few words in that strange language and snaps his fingers. Before my eyes, the spool transforms back into a bale of hay. "You know your punishment." He gestures to the beam, casts another charm, and a pile of thick, black rope coils at my feet.

"Please," I whisper. "What the King asked—it is impossible. Only one of the Fae can turn straw into gold. You cannot possibly punish me for this."

"Oh, but I will. The Fae always keep our promises." The Prince tucks a lock of hair behind my ear, and I try not to recoil, but when his hand lingers on my neck, part of me wants to lean closer. He is working his charms on me, and my addled mind teeters on the edge of control. "Perhaps you would be interested in a bargain to escape your punishment?"

No. Not again.

Yet, with him touching me, his magic curling around me, I find myself saying, "What are your terms?"

"I will tell my Father you only needed a bit of instruction. That under my guidance, you spun one of the bales into gold and you can do the rest given another day. That you can spin even more. That will stay your punishment. Perhaps I will even waive it entirely." The Prince's fingers gently massage my neck. "You need a bath, Lia. Fresh clothing. Care. I could give you all of that."

"And...what would I have to give in return?" My voice is barely audible, and I try to focus on my memories of Roarke. Of how he held me all night, of how his strong arms felt wrapped around me.

"I love you. And I will free you."

The Prince's words are right in my ear, and he continues to massage my neck. "There are many types of Fae. Did you know that, my Lia?"

The Prince shifts me closer to him, his fingers rough and no longer as comforting. His touch feels so very different than Roarke's that my addled brain starts to focus. I cannot allow myself to be bound any further. Not when Roarke promised to come back for me.

"I only know what I have seen," I whisper. "You. Your cruel father. The guards who hold the town hostage…"

"Hostage? No. We protect you."

I choke out a laugh. "Protect us? We cannot leave. The outcasts work our whole lives for nothing." Anger strengthens me, and I sit up taller and turn my hands palms up. "I cannot feel anything with three of my fingers, *Prince*. Because I have been spinning wool since I was old enough to operate the spindle. Because my father drinks to forget he is trapped here. That he helped create *me* and trap *me* here as well."

The Prince's face holds no emotion at all, but his voice… that is full of understanding. Fake understanding. "We draw energy from suffering. It gives us life. Eternal life." His shoulders straighten. "I am fifty-three years old, Lia. Yet, I look as if I am twenty."

Shock leaves me speechless, which is probably a good thing, as I feel his influence pressing down on my free will.

"If I take away your punishment, I ask only one thing." The Prince cups my cheek.

Why did I think his touch was so terrible?

"What?"

"Kiss me." He leans closer. For a moment, I see Roarke's face, but then I blink, and the eyes that hold mine are the wrong color. They should be deep hazel with bright amber flecks, and they are not. Silver irises, so pale they are almost white stare back at me. His face changes too, his cheeks no longer chiseled and broad, his nose narrow and almost hooked. After another blink, it shifts again, his mask back in place. But I have seen behind it now. I cannot kiss him. I *will* not kiss him. Not ever. Not willingly.

Roarke will come for me. I can endure whatever pain the Prince subjects me to if I can only see him again.

I shove the Prince back hard enough that his head hits the edge of my cot. "I would sooner die than feel your lips on mine. Do what you want to me, *Prince*. I will never be yours."

"Guards!" His shout brings the three large Fae bursting into the room. "Strip her."

CHAPTER NINE

AURELIA

I scream as the tallest guard pins me down, sitting on my thighs as the darker-haired one ties my wrists together and hands the end of the rope to the Prince. He pulls my arms over my head so I cannot sit up or fight.

My leather corset rips under their hands, followed by my blouse, and then my breasts are bared to the cold morning air. My skirt is next, yanked down my hips and tossed away. Lastly, they unlace my boots and pull off my thin woolen stockings and panties.

"Now what?" one of them asks the Prince.

"Bring her to my chambers," he says.

The tallest one wraps the rope around his fist and nods his head towards the door. "Walk or be dragged."

"I will walk," I say and struggle to my feet. The trek to the Prince's chambers is long. Down a long stone stairway, then through an ornately decorated hall with golden carvings, beautiful paintings, and statues set into alcoves. Finally, up another stairway where there are two doors—one to the right and the other to the left.

The door on the right is open, and the guard pulls me through a lavish parlor with two chaises, a rich, dark wood table polished to a high shine, and oil lamps burning brightly.

"In here," the Prince calls. "She will do her time bound where I can appreciate her body."

His bedroom. No.

I dig in my heels, the soft rugs covering the floor giving me a small bit of purchase. But the guards are too big, too strong, and they simply pull me until I fall to my knees and drag me the rest of the way.

"Bind her properly now," he says with a wave of his hand.

The tall guard tosses the rope over a horizontal beam in the ceiling and pulls my arms up until I am forced up onto the balls of my feet against the hard wooden beam. Another long rope winds around my waist to just under my breasts, and yet another binds my legs from mid-thighs to just below my knees.

My most intimate areas are left bare as I face the Prince's bed, and the bastard lounges against numerous pillows piled on his unmade bed, watching me. "This is better, Lia. Is it not? You are mine, after all. Leaving you alone in that tower room? Unacceptable. I should not have done that to my future bride."

"I am *not* your future bride," I whisper.

"Oh, but you are, my sweet Lia." He chuckles and lifts a pitcher from the table on the side of his bed, then pours amber liquid into a glass. "It is only a matter of time before you accept your fate."

Sauntering over to me, he holds the glass to my lips, but I shake my head. "You are drugging me. I would rather die."

Anger flares in his eyes and he pinches my nose shut,

then forces the nectar down my throat. "You will submit to me, Lia. Or you will beg for a death that will never be granted."

Once I swallow enough of the liquid for his satisfaction, he cups my cheek and rests two fingers against my temple. "What do you want, Lia? What is your greatest desire?"

"To be free of you." The words escape on a hiss. My entire body warms, despite the chill in the room, and I fight against the pull of the charmed drink. I am so very hungry and still thirsty after all the tears I cried the previous day. My feet ache, and whenever I try to relax them for a bit of relief, the ropes bite painfully into my wrists.

The Prince tosses the empty glass onto the bed so he can grab my head in both of his hands. He pries my eyes open when I try to close them, and his stare bores into me. "You are mine, Lia. Nothing will ever change that."

"I am...not...yours."

"Oh, but you are." He touches his forehead to mine. "Yet you desire another."

I gasp and jerk my head back, slamming it into the beam. Splinters dig into my scalp, but the pain helps me focus and dispel the effects of whatever magic the Fae impart through food and drink.

How does he know?

With a roll of his eyes, the Prince presses his palms to my temples once more. "This other male...he is not Fae. He does not stand a chance against us."

I cannot betray the man who vowed to save me. Forcing my mind to go blank, I hold onto my rage, my hatred of the Fae and everything they are. "Can you hear my thoughts now, you bloody bastard?"

Die, you piece of excrement. If you had any redeeming qualities at all, you would not have to trick a woman and force her to become your bride. You may own my body because of your father's trickery, but you will never have my love. Nor any of my respect.

The Prince grabs my jaw, leans in, and presses his lips to mine. I scream against his kiss, flailing against the ropes binding me in any way I can, but they are too tight. This is wrong. So very wrong. Everything in me knows this is not the man I am supposed to be with, but when he forces his tongue inside my mouth, I hear his words in my head.

"You are my bride, Lia. And you will stay with me forever."

I have no tears left to cry, but my eyes burn all the same. The Prince is right. I will be trapped here for the rest of my days. And Roarke—*No!* I cannot let myself think of anything but how much I hate the Prince in this moment. Not if he can hear my thoughts.

Except when I close my eyes, I see a strong, graceful dragon flying away from the tower, and when I open them again, the Prince is gone, and I fear I have just condemned not only my own soul, but Roarke's as well.

THE PRINCE LEAVES me bound to the beam facing his bed long enough my body goes numb. He has returned a handful of times, always with a bit of honeyed cake or cured meat or some of the charmed nectar that makes me feel strange. Like something is waking up inside of me, aching to be released.

Each time he tries to be sweet. To show me he is something other than completely evil. But though his words are calming, soft, and reassuring, his thoughts bleed through. We have some sort of connection—either that or I have lost my mind completely—and I can hear him whispering to me between the words he says aloud.

"What is your name?"

It is foolish. The Fae have the power to read minds. Humans do not. But I have to try something. Anything.

"I could release you, sweet Lia," he says as he offers me a strawberry. I am beyond refusing food, even though I feel his influence over me asserting itself with each bite. "Bathe you." He waves his hand, and a gust of wind opens another door I have been staring at all day.

The deep, stone tub wrenches a moan from my chapped lips. Steam wafts from the water within, and my aching muscles scream at me for relief.

"I am prepared to die bound to this beam," I mumble, my tongue too thick for my mouth. "Nothing you will ever say will convince me to love you."

"You will change your mind," he declares as he strokes a hand over my hair. "I am a reasonable man, Lia." He loosens the knots that bind me and catches me when I fall. My wrists are still tied, but he gathers the excess rope and carries me to the stone tub.

My muscles scream as he sets me in the hot water, and though he binds my hands to a hasp secured to the wall, he does not otherwise touch me.

"The water is heated by Fae magic. It will remain at this temperature for hours."

I am so thankful for the chance to rest, to be warm, that I do not protest when he helps me lean back and washes my hair.

Nor when he wraps me in a towel.

Nor when he—for a moment—unbinds me and slides a white silk dress over my body. It clings to my curves and brushes my sore, bare feet.

Nor when he ties the ropes around my wrists again and then knots the end of the rope around his ornately carved headboard. "Rest, my sweet Lia. And think of me when you dream."

The compulsion to sleep is so strong, and I am so tired and sore and completely without hope that I give in. Even though I am in his bed with his scent striking a discordant tone that skitters along my spine and threatens to drive me mad.

"*What is your name?*" As I drift off, I try again, and just before I slip under, I think I hear a mumbled reply. But I cannot understand the Prince's response. I close my eyes and let the darkness swallow my fears that soon, I will actually start to care for this monster.

CHAPTER TEN

I have visited close to one hundred cottages and shacks since I left Aurelia in that godforsaken tower, and I am no closer to finding out that bastard Prince's name.

In desperation, I show up on Crux's doorstep. "I need to speak to the drunkard."

"Roarke, you must stop this foolishness," Crux replies. "He is a fool, and you are risking your life over a human woman you will never be allowed to marry. Every magic bearer who comes to this realm tries to fight the Fae and we have all failed. Are you so unhappy here you are determined to die?"

Shoving Crux against the wall, I let my beast rise close to the surface. He can see it in my eyes. How deadly I can be. A low growl rumbles through my chest. "She is my mate."

"Fuck me. You're a shifter."

"And you are a bloody fool. Any warlock worth his salt should have been able to sense that."

Crux holds up his hands, trying to force some space between us. "I didn't try, mate. We all have our secrets here."

I peer down at him, unsure what I might have missed about him given the semi-smug look on his face.

"I'm a Druid," he says quietly. "One of the ancients."

"And still you cannot escape?" Taking a step back, I force myself to calm. If he is as he claims, perhaps we can work together if—when—I free Aurelia.

"My magic depends on my connection to the physical world. But this realm..." He runs a hand through his hair as he leads me into the kitchen towards the stove and the trapdoor. "The essence of every living thing here is controlled and manipulated by the Fae. They take so much, there is little left for me to tap into. Outside the veil, I could command mountains. Inside, I am lucky to be able to tumble a single rock down a hill."

He pushes the stove away from the wall. "You are certain this human is your mate?"

"Yes. The connection I feel to her is unmistakable. And she is not entirely human. Her father—" I stop, holding Crux's gaze, trying to impress upon him the importance of what I am about to say. "Her father was one of the Fae guards. She is part Fae, and if she can tap into her power..."

"Fuck me." Crux shakes his head. "Then talk to the idiot. And when you are done, tell me what I can do to help." He mutters to himself as he opens the trapdoor, believing me more of a fool than Abbot. I probably am, but I will not stop until Aurelia is free or I am dead. If Abbot knows anything, he will tell me or suffer my dragon's wrath.

"Abbot! You had better have information for me," I yell as I stomp down the stairs.

He huddles on the thin pallet of blankets, his arms around his shins, his knees drawn up. "If I do, it is yours."

Smart man.

"The Prince. What do you know of him?"

"N-nothing." Abbot shakes his head, his brows furrowing in confusion. "I have never seen him without the King. He always comes to Aurelia's stall on Market day, usually for a pair of socks—which he demands for free, of course—and asks her questions. But she knows not to engage the Fae. I taught her that from an early age. Sometimes they take more valuable wares, and she keeps a few items hidden away in case they are ever dissatisfied with what she offers them."

"Have you ever heard his name?"

With a shake of his head, Abbot runs a hand through his thinning, gray hair. "No. My...June said that the Fae guard their names carefully. They only speak them to one another and never where a human could hear."

"Fuck." I punch the stone wall, breaking four knuckles in a single blow. My dragon roars at the pain, and when I release a bit of my hold on him, he huffs, and steam escapes my lips. The injury heals quickly—in less than the time it took me to descend the stairs—and I start to pace the small room.

"Aurelia will never be free until she can tell the bastard Prince she does not love him—using his name. Until then, she will very likely spend her entire captivity bound, beaten, and terrorized. I will *not* let that happen."

Abbot chokes back a sob. "This is all my fault."

"Yes, you dolt. It is." I run my hands through my long, black hair and pull tightly on the strands. I must return to Aurelia soon. If the Prince truly has her bound to that beam, she has been there all day in terrible pain.

I shed my coat and dig in a leather bag I retrieved from my cottage earlier in the day—the one I haven't used since the Fae magic trapped me here. I'd been on my way from Greenland to the wilds of Alaska where I'd last seen my brothers. This bag held all of my earthly possessions at the time. Several changes of clothing, some gold, and...fuck me. How could I have forgotten?

Under one of my journals left inside, under the last few gold coins I never traded away, I find my belt. The iron studs are purely decorative, but there are enough of them I might be able to use them—somehow.

"Wait," Abbot peers up at me, his eyes wide. "You said 'bastard Prince.'"

"Yes. He is. The King never claimed a mate." One by one, I pop the iron bolts from the leather and tuck them into a small pocket inside the bag.

"June's final Market day, she saw the King and the Prince walking among the people. There were whispers of 'the bastard Prince.' But that night, June told me the Prince wasn't a bastard. She spent two nights in the Fae tower with her lover, and he used his glamour to hide her when they walked the halls."

"Is there a point to this?" Dusk is close, and every second I spend away from Aurelia is pure agony.

"She saw another human. A woman. On the King's arm. And the Prince? Looks just like her."

At the edge of the forest, I once more strip out of my clothing, fold it carefully, and tuck it all into the leather bag. Naked, the early autumn breeze tickles my skin, and I stare up at the tower. At Aurelia's window.

I am coming for you, my darling. We will survive this. Together.

My dragon takes flight, the leather bag clutched in his

talons. Exhaustion presses down on me, and I struggle to maintain the magic that hides me from Fae eyes. Our landing on the tower roof is nowhere near as graceful as it was the previous night, and I cringe as my beast relinquishes control and I shift back into a man. I only pause long enough to pull on my pants and shoes before securing the leather strap to the capstone and rappelling down to Aurelia's window.

The moment I land in a crouch in the tower room, I know something is very, very wrong. Her scent has faded, and that of a male Fae lingers. The fucking Prince.

When I see her clothing torn to shreds on the stone floor, rage consumes me. My dragon whines, desperate to take control and destroy everything and everyone that had a part in her pain.

If she is not here, she is with *him*. My mind reels. He could be torturing her. Or worse. Touching her. Convincing her to mate with him.

No. I will not lose her.

Jamming my hand under the thin mattress, I find the bag of iron shavings. She did not use them.

"He fed me this sweet nectar. And then I could no longer think clearly. I started to wonder...would it really be that bad here?

Fuck. He turned her. Fed her, drugged her, and charmed her into loving him.

Except, I can still sense Aurelia. Her heart. We are still linked in some way, so she has not completely turned to his side.

"Aurelia, my darling. Can you hear me?" I sling my bag over my shoulder and stride for the door. It opens easily at my touch, revealing a long hallway with oil lamps every few feet. Letting my dragon take control, I scent my mate and head to the left.

"Roarke! Run!" Her terrorized scream sends my heart

leaping into my throat, and my dragon roars so loudly, it shakes the tower walls. He's so close to the surface, my skin starts to shift into dark green scales along the backs of my hands, and sharp talons extend from my fingers.

At the top of the stairs, the Prince holds Aurelia against him. Her hands are bound, and his fingers wrap around her throat. Her white silk gown leaves little to the imagination, and my anger flares white hot.

"Let. Her. Go," I shout as I reach for the dagger. But the talons make gripping anything difficult, and I come away empty handed. Before I can try again, men who feel more like gargoyles than Fae slam into me from behind, and I go down, hard. Fists rain over my back, and I let my dragon take control.

He snorts and tries to burn the Fae, but shifting takes precious minutes, and as my bones pop and crack, something snaps around my neck. My body goes ice cold. It's as if my dragon has been torn away, ripped from my being and murdered before my eyes.

I howl in pain, and I'm drowning in the loss of my other half, as vital to me as air. He's left me with broken bones, scales that turn black as pitch in a single breath, and no strength in my limbs.

Manacles wrap around my wrists, pinning them behind me, and then the guards roll me over and continue to kick and pummel me as Aurelia screams.

"Let him go! Please!" she begs. "He is no threat to you. I cannot leave this place. Ever. You have seen to that! Let him live!"

"He is a *dragon*, my sweet Lia. His magic? It will give us power for centuries. Perhaps even allow us to leave this realm and return to our own. With you. Of course."

"I will accept you!" She turns and grabs his vest. "If you release him, we can be married before the sun sets."

"No! Aurelia, no!" My voice is hoarse and weak, and I use my legs to push my prone body towards the stairs. The guards stand back and let me try to reach her, which should terrify me, but all I can think about is Aurelia.

Blood drips into my eyes, and I cannot wipe it away. Aurelia's gaze locks onto mine, and the sorrow and regret in those hazel depths tear what's left of my heart into pieces.

The Prince grabs her by the hair and drags her down the stairs behind him. Her legs scramble for purchase, and she claws at his fingers with her bound hands.

"If you harm her," I growl as the guards haul me up and slam me against the wall, "I will gut you."

"I would like to see you try," the Prince says, throwing Aurelia at my feet. She tries to rise, but he presses his booted foot down on her back and she whimpers my name. Her fingers graze my ankle, and a spark races through me at the contact.

But then the Prince shifts his foot onto her hands, and she screams as a bone snaps.

With a lecherous grin, the Prince punches me in the stomach. "Take him to the dungeon and ensure his *beast* is well contained. My father and I will be down as soon as I teach my future bride a lesson about what happens when she keeps secrets from me."

As they drag me away, I have to watch the Prince lift Aurelia to her feet and press a kiss to her broken fingers. She's shaking violently, and I call her name, over and over again, hoping for one more moment of connection. But the Prince turns her away from me, and all I hear is her sobbing, "I am sorry. So sorry," over and over again.

~

THE TALL FAE GUARDS—BOTH with long blond hair and features that should not exist outside fine art—throw me down flight after flight of stairs, and without my dragon to protect and heal me, I break several ribs, my ankle, and my nose. One of my shoulders dislocates, and I stifle my scream. I will not give them the satisfaction of hearing my pain.

Thirty floors later, I smell the damp earth. We are underground now, and I can barely hold on to consciousness. The guards uncuff me, but they are too quick, and fasten chains around both wrists. I pass out when my dislocated shoulder pops back into place, and when I wake again, my arms and legs are spread wide and my clothing is gone. The metal collar burns, its charm now in full control of my body.

I was wrong before. My dragon is not dead. He has not left me completely. But when I reach for him, I hear only pained whines, and I *feel* nothing. My beast is a part of me. Has been since the day I was born. But now...he languishes just out of reach, begging me to free him before death claims us both.

If only I could.

I will die here. My leather bag is gone. I cannot remember if the guards took it or if it slipped off my shoulder when I ran for Aurelia.

My entire body is consumed by frigid fire, burning and freezing me at the same time. I know only agony and pain, and even focusing on my mate for the briefest moment will soon become impossible.

By the time the Prince and the King come for me, I fear Aurelia will already be lost. And if not, they will torture me and use my pain to force her to submit. To bind herself to them forever.

I let my head hang down, the charmed metal digging into my throat. Each breath is harder than the last, and I think perhaps...it would be better if I simply died now. Stopped fighting and slipped away.

Then, at least they would not be able to take my power.

But that is the curse of being immortal. Unless my head is severed from my body or my heart is cut out completely, I will live. And every second from now until eternity promises nothing but pain.

CHAPTER ELEVEN

AURELIA

When the Prince came for me, I was still asleep in his bed. My dreams were full of Roarke. All the times he visited my stall on Market days. The jokes he would tell to make me laugh. The single time I risked going on a picnic with him in the forest. His scent.

And his dragon. Flying away from my tower prison with such grace after promising to return the next night.

My own dreams betrayed me.

"You little harlot!" the Prince shouts as he jerks me up by my bound wrists and hauls me out of his bed so quickly, I land on the floor. *"Your rescuer is here. I think you should watch as I destroy him."*

My mind is so addled from sleep and thoughts of Roarke that I do not understand until the Prince drags me out the door of his chambers and to the top of the stairs. There, he picks me up and sets me on my aching feet, then wraps his fingers around my throat.

That is the moment I sense Roarke.

I cannot see him yet, but I know he is close. "Roarke! Run!"

The Prince tightens his grip. Not enough to hurt me, but enough to let me know he could cut off all of my air so easily. I claw at his hands, but he merely uses the rope to pull my arms away.

And then I see the man I think...I know...I have fallen in love with.

The Prince makes me watch. Forces me. I try to close my eyes when the guards start beating my love, but then I hear the Prince's words in my head—a command I cannot ignore.

"You will open your eyes."

And I do.

The small bites of food, the nectar...I have felt weaker each time. As if my mind—my thoughts—are slowly becoming his. He can control my body with only his words now?

He pulls me down the stairs, not caring that I lose my footing, and when he tells the guards to take Roarke away, he nudges my chin up and forces me to look in his eyes. "That collar, my sweet Lia, binds his dragon. He cannot fight our charms, and we will draw upon his power for all eternity in the most painful way possible," the Prince sneers. "He is powerless. This is what you pine for? How can you want that when you have me?"

HE LEADS me back to his chambers, and I follow meekly. What is the use of fighting any longer? Roarke will die, and I will become the Prince's bride. My broken fingers throb with every beat of my heart. If this is how he treats a woman he is courting, my life as his bride will be so much worse.

"You must serve the rest of your punishment now, Lia," he says patiently as he hands me over to his two personal guards. They push me against the beam, only this time, they angle me so the hard corner of the beam digs into my back. Ropes lash me from just under my breasts to my knees. My breaths are shallow; I'm tied too tightly to inhale deeply.

The Prince strokes my cheek with a finger, then dashes away one of my tears.

"You are a monster," I hiss.

With a small shake of his head, he glances at the guards. One of them digs his fingers into the hinge of my jaw while the other forces a thick piece of cloth between my teeth, then ties it around the beam, pinning my head to the sharp edge and gagging me at the same time.

"That is for your foul tongue." He leans in and brushes his lips to mine. Looking me up and down, he sighs and lifts my bound hands. "I do apologize for these."

My scream is muffled by the gag as he squeezes my broken fingers, and my vision turns glassy.

"I never meant to harm you, Lia. You must believe me. You do, yes?" Touching his forehead to mine, he repeats his words, only this time, he does not speak aloud. *"You believe me. I never meant to harm you. If you had not disobeyed, you would not have been hurt."*

"If I had not disobeyed, I would not have been hurt."

Deep inside, I know that is a lie. But I cannot help myself from agreeing with him. From trying to nod my head, even though it is a futile gesture bound as I am. The Prince smiles at me, and his face transforms into something beautiful.

It is all a lie.

My heart knows this, even though my eyes deceive me. He tosses the end of the rope to the guards, and they raise my hands over my head, tying a knot to a hasp well out of my reach. The movement thrusts my breasts forward, and in the cool air of the room, my nipples pebble under the thin white silk.

"You are a vision like this," the Prince says. "Your pain is intoxicating. I could live off of it for centuries. And I will." He kisses the tears from my cheeks, and I cry more for him, unable to stop, which only makes his influence over me stronger.

"By the time I return, Lia, you will have forgotten all about the dragon."

The guards leave, followed by the Prince, and my head pounds, my thoughts at war with one another. Nothing makes sense to me, least of all, the Prince's words.

What dragon?

~

ROARKE

The Fae move so silently, I don't hear the King and the Prince enter the room. Then again, I can only hear my own thready heartbeat in my ears. The guards have not moved from their stations at the door, and I have remained silent.

I pour every ounce of energy I have left into sensing Aurelia. The tether between us is frightfully tenuous, but it has not frayed completely.

Aurelia, please, my darling. You must find what is hidden deep inside you.

A small spark warms me, but only for a moment, because the King grabs a chunk of my hair and pulls my head back to meet his gaze. "A dragon in our very midst. How fortuitous."

"Fuck you." I spit in his face, and he steps back and wipes his cheek with a chuckle, then nods at the guards.

"You may begin."

The snap of a whip is quickly followed by blazing pain licking across my back. They strike time and time again, until my skin splits and blood runs down my naked body.

Pain can be overcome. I send my mind soaring above the trees, my dragon in control. My brothers, Kipling, Camdyn, and Dameon, rise up to meet me, and we play as younglings over the wildlands that are now part of Alaska.

I have not seen them in a century, and I ache to know if they are even still alive. We were hunted for so long, separated, and alone. Until I'd heard their call.

I stay in this dream for hours, only dimly aware of what is going on around me. I know the guards have moved on to other forms of torture. I can vaguely sense the temperature in the room dropping, blunt impact to my thighs, my ribs. But walling off my mind keeps the worst of the agony at bay. The wind ruffles my hair as I soar over the tops of trees and dip down to skim a wing tip through the water.

Whatever happens to me now, I will endure until the end, and perhaps then, I will find peace.

CHAPTER TWELVE

AURELIA

The sun streams through the Prince's window, and still, I remain bound. He slumbers in the bed, close enough I can hear his snores.

I caught fragments of sleep between the hours of agony, but each time, I jerked awake to feel his hands on me. Cupping my cheek, kissing away my tears.

A day has passed, I think. Or most of one, since he ordered me tied here.

Several times, I have dreamed of a massive dragon. Four of them, actually. One, I recognize. I know he is mine, even if the Prince has done his best to force me to forget him. His name... why can I not remember his name?

I must make some sound, because the Prince opens his eyes and smiles at me. I hate that smile. Hate him. Yet, a piece of me longs for him and I do not know why. "You are awake, my sweet Lia," the Prince says, rising and moving towards me. He is naked, and I blink hard as his body seems to fuzz in and out of focus.

When he reaches my side, he kisses my cheek, then whispers a few words that cause the ropes and the gag to fall away.

I fall as well. My limbs are numb; I am too weak to move, too weak to do anything but cry out as my broken fingers send shocks of pain up my left arm. "Now, now, Lia. Is that any way to greet your future husband?"

My mouth is so dry, I cannot speak, but I gaze up at him with all the hatred I can muster. His pale, spindly arms and legs seem so different when he is clothed. Bulkier. Stronger. His nose has changed as well. Sharp and angled, almost hooked. His chin is weak and even his hair is not the same. No longer thick and tumbling over his shoulders, it resembles poorly spun thread, and there is a greasy shine to it.

"The Fae have the power to make themselves look beautiful at all times," my grandmother says as she sits across from me at our small table. "You must always try to see past their disguises to the beings inside."

I blink, hard, and the Prince's visage changes back to the handsome—if not vile—man I have seen for the past three— or is it four now?—days. But when I repeat the motion, his mask falls away, revealing the ugliness both inside and out.

Am I truly resisting him? If so...how?

He lifts me in his arms and sets me on the bed. "You have completed the punishment for failing to spin the straw into gold. There is still the matter of your errant thoughts, and your deception. Hiding the dragon from me will earn you much pain. But I think we will delay that for a time. Perhaps until after we are married."

That damnable cup of nectar presses to my lips, and I shake my head. "Not thirsty," I manage, even though I am certain I cannot go much longer without water.

"Yes. You are." He presses his hand over my heart. "You are very thirsty, Lia. You are desperate for what I will give you."

The sensation builds until it feels like he is ripping a piece of my mind from my head and the thought of *not* drinking tears me apart, but still manage a weak "no."

"She dares refuse me?"

His words are as clear to me as if he spoke them aloud, but I know he did not because his lips are pressed into a thin line.

"What have you done with him?" I search my mind for my dragon's name. He is my mate. He loves me. He told me there was something inside me I needed to find. "Where is Roarke?"

My triumph at defeating the Prince's charms is short-lived. He laughs, throwing his head back in a full-body chortle that makes my blood run cold.

"You were, perhaps, hoping to be rescued, Lia?" he asks as he banishes the cup with a wave of his hand. "I think not. Your only hope, the pitiful creature you *think* you love, is completely under our control, and I believe you need to see just what that means."

Yes. Bring me to Roarke. Let me see him.

The Prince throws me over his shoulder and carries me down so many flights of stairs, by the time we reach the bottom, I want to vomit from the incessant pounding in my head. A heavy stone door scrapes open, and I hear the King's voice.

"Take another piece."

A piece? Of what?

I do not have to wait long for the Prince to set me on my feet so I can see my worst nightmares come to life.

Blood covers the floor. Spatters, long streaks, and a pool directly under my mate's ravaged body. One of the King's men, a large Fae with pointed ears and a scar running down the side of his face, takes a silver blade and slides it along Roarke's upper thigh. A thin layer of skin peels off as I slap my hand over my mouth in horror. An inhuman wail escapes his throat, hoarse and weak, and he jerks against the chains holding him.

A burst of strength infuses my limbs, and I spring for my dragon, slipping on the blood, but managing to wrap my arms around his waist. "Roarke," I whisper in his ear. "Fight this. Please. Let your dragon destroy them."

Another guard wrenches me away from him, and something buried deep inside me breaks free. Roarke meets my gaze, and his bloodshot eyes widen. "Aurelia," he whispers. His voice fades away, or shifts somehow, and then he's in my head. *"Hide your power from them. Now!"*

His head drops and his entire body sags in his chains as I'm thrust back towards the Prince, and I shutter my thoughts, putting a lid on my rage and doing my best to appear completely and totally broken.

It is not difficult. Sobs tear from my throat, as the Prince grips my arms so tightly, he will certainly leave bruises. The King tips my head up, and I cry harder, hoping my tears obscure the hatred in my eyes.

"Your dragon's pain is the strongest we have ever felt. We could easily kill him. Take out his heart. But why when we can keep him alive for all eternity and make him suffer every single day?" He strides over to Roarke, taking the knife from the guard and thrusting it deep into my dragon's side.

"We will use him as an example for all the people of the realm. Bind him in the center of the Market and bring him to the brink of death over and over again. Such a powerful warning against ever lying to the Fae."

"Please, stop this," I beg. "I will fulfill my bargain. There is no need—"

The King snarls as he passes the blade back to the guard and stalks towards me again. "I could flay all of the skin from his body—and may very well do so—because of your disobedience. His pain? All of it? Is on your head."

"No," I sob. "I will not resist. I will marry your son tonight if you will release Roarke unharmed."

"Nothing will stop the Prince from taking you as his mate, you foolish girl. I have no reason to even allow you to voice your demands. Return her to her room, my son. Then it is your turn to siphon the pure, unadulterated pain from this wretched creature."

The King turns away, dismissing me, and I lose control, screaming obscenities as I kick the Prince in the balls, then jump on the King's back and wrap my arm around his throat. He sputters, wheezing, and stumbles, but with a wave of his hand, all of the air is sucked out of the room, and I am the one who falls to the floor clutching my chest.

Roarke's pale lips start to turn blue, and his entire body convulses in his chains. My vision darkens, and just before I pass out, the air is returned, and I suck in a loud, shuddering breath. The Prince's guards take me—one pinning my wrists together in his hands, the other holding my ankles, and carry me from the room as Roarke screams my name.

BACK IN MY TOWER PRISON, I curl on my side, breathing in shallow pants. The guards kicked me so hard, I think one of my ribs is broken. They shackled my right wrist to my left ankle around the beam with only a very short chain, so I can do nothing but lie on the floor or sit hunched over.

The Prince forced more nectar down my throat not long ago, but though I feigned appreciation—and submission—I felt neither. Whatever new power now lives within me is awake and very angry. The Prince's thoughts are as clear as glass, and I can even hear others in the stone tower, though they are so far away—and so numerous—I cannot discern individual words.

I must find a way to escape and get to Roarke. The first two fingers on my left hand are useless, and moving the others causes me intense pain. The shackles require a key that I do not have, and from this position, I can only reach the chamber pot they left for me, the shredded remnants of my corset, and a few broken pieces of straw.

Closing my eyes, I strain to focus on everything I hear, but even though the nectar can no longer convince me the Prince is anything but pure evil, it can still tempt my broken body with sleep and muddle my thoughts.

But then, I hear one tremulous female voice. *"Let me in. Can you not see I have medical supplies and food? I am the King's consort, you stupid brutes."*

When the door creaks open, I try to wriggle around to see who is coming, but the pain in my ribs threatens to steal my consciousness.

The hands that flit over my shoulders shake, and a soft, sorrowful sound comes from the woman's throat. She helps me to sit up, and then unbuttons her cloak and wraps it around me. It is cold in this room, even with the sun up, and I only wear the bloodstained sleeveless silk gown. No undergarments, no shoes. My boots are halfway across the room.

"Th-thank you," I say. She's human, that much I know. Her flaming red hair, green eyes, and the various bruises covering the left side of her face leave no doubt in my mind. Next to her, there's a tray with a glass of what looks like water—actual water—that she presses into my free hand.

More proof she is not Fae.

"Who are you?" I ask when I have drained half the glass and feel almost alert for the first time since the Prince first forced that damn nectar down my throat.

The woman shakes her head and parts her lips.

I gasp, then regret the motion as my ribs send pain wrapping around my torso. Her tongue is mostly gone.

"He did that to you. The King?" I whisper, and she nods.

"I hate him. I wish I could kill him."

Reaching for the woman's hand, I forget my broken fingers for a moment. "I can kill him."

She jerks back, wide eyed.

"I can hear your thoughts. I don't know how. But if you can get me out of these shackles, I might have a chance. He has a dragon chained below ground. *My* dragon. I need to free him. Then...maybe..." Speaking exhausts me, every breath sending pain wrapping around my torso.

"You are Fae."

"No. No, no, no," I wheeze. I cannot be Fae. I will not entertain the notion that I can be anything like these vile creatures. But the woman nods.

"You are the spinner's daughter. She fell in love with one of the King's own guards. I remember her being in the castle, though the guard tried to keep her hidden. My name is Noelle. I may be able to help you."

The woman—Noelle—pulls up her skirt to reveal a dagger strapped to her thigh. Nausea claws its way up my throat.

"Where did you get that?"

"I am the King's consort. The Prince...he is my son. One of them. The other..." She shakes her head, tears shining in her eyes. Quickly, she unbuckles the holster and pushes up my dress. I nod, and she fastens the straps around my right leg. As soon as the blade touches my skin, it burns, and I cry out.

Iron is deadly to the Fae, and though I want to deny what I am, this is proof. Can I even wield the weapon?

Noelle holds a finger to her lips, then picks up a piece of my leather corset, wrapping it around my leg to keep the poisonous metal from directly touching my skin.

"Th-thank you," I whisper. "But I cannot do anything bound as I am. When the Prince comes, he is never alone, and he will charm me before I have a chance to use the dagger."

She smiles and plucks a hairpin from the knot of red curls atop her head. The locks fall away in under a minute. Clearly, she has had to do this before.

Even with the leather protecting my skin, the dagger still burns, but it has shifted to a dull ache, and I can bear it if there is a chance I can earn my freedom.

"Can you teach me how to do that?" I ask. "I have to free Roarke. The collar they put on him...it lets them siphon his pain...forever. His dragon cannot escape it, and they are torturing him."

Noelle tenses and glances back at the door. *"We do not have much time. The chains will be charmed. The only way to break them is with iron."*

Freed, I crawl over to the narrow cot and shove my hand under the mattress. The bag of shavings is still there, and I thrust it at Noelle. "Will these help?"

She nods. *"Yes. With these, and this,"* she tells me, holding up her hairpin, *"I should be able to help him get free. But there are still the two guards outside."*

I swallow hard. "Leave them to me. But there is one other matter. I cannot leave this place—this castle—until I can say the Prince's name and tell him I do not love him. But I do not know what his name is."

Pain pinches her tired features, and she shakes her head.

"Before the King took my tongue, he and his mage wove a charm that wiped my own son's name from my head. If I even try to remember..." She wavers on her knees, and her skin pales. *"I would give anything to be able to help you. But that...you must do alone."*

CHAPTER THIRTEEN

I curl on the cold stone, the shackles draped over my wrist and ankle, but no longer locked, and the dagger clutched in my uninjured hand.

Noelle screams and flings open the door, grabbing for the arm of one of the Fae guards and trying to pull him into the room. She points to me frantically, then clutches her throat.

"What is it, consort?" the guard asks as he approaches me. She jabs me in the chest, and I do not move, and now, I can sense his apprehension. When he leans down to touch my neck, I strike, driving the blade into his belly and twisting sharply.

He tries to call out, and his partner races into the room just as Noelle slams the door to keep their screams from reaching any other ears. Leaping to my feet, I charge the second guard.

"Do not fight me." I send every ounce of my mental energy towards him, hoping perhaps these new powers of mine are strong enough to work on a pure-bred Fae.

He lifts his hand and his mouth opens, but he hesitates for a single moment. Long enough for me to slash at his throat.

Crimson sprays across my chest, and he gurgles as he sinks to his knees. Both guards struggle to get up, but the second is losing blood at an alarming rate, and the first... His innards spill into one of his hands as he rises.

"You will pay for that," he says hoarsely.

"I think not." I plunge the dagger into his chest, then take a single step back as his eyes roll back in his head and he takes his final breath, falling onto his partner.

I have just killed two of the Fae. If I do not escape now, I have sentenced myself to a death more horrible than I can possibly imagine. But more importantly, I know I can affect their minds. While I doubt my ability to compel anyone, especially the Prince, even if I can merely distract them for a moment or two, that power—and the dagger in my hand—could be enough to win my freedom.

Now to see just how strong my powers are. I have to find the Prince and see if I can invade his mind. If so, perhaps I can trick him into telling me his name.

ROARKE

Time means nothing to me now. The King and the Prince have toyed with me for so long, I can no longer stand. The manacles bite into my wrists, and my dragon...he prays for death. But he did not see Aurelia's eyes.

For one brief moment, the power of the Fae flowed through her veins, and if I had been able to call upon my dragon, we might have been able to leave this place. Together.

I will languish here forever. But my mate...she has a chance to be free. Will I know? Of course I will. If she is wed to the Prince, they will parade her in front of me, use her to amplify my pain, and use me to torment her.

The guards sit in the corner of the room, occasionally pointing and laughing at me, but the King and the Prince left some time ago. An hour. Maybe two? I can only tell by how the last few wounds have nearly stopped bleeding.

My skin burns, my shoulders ache, and a flea has more strength than I do. But I will never give these bastards the satisfaction of seeing me break. I could no longer wall off my mind when they began to flay the skin from my body, but the rest...I can endure.

I force my head up as one of the guards curses viciously, then falls to the floor with his hands around his throat, choking. A woman with hair the color of a dying fire holds out her hand and the other guard backs away. "What are you doing?" he asks.

The woman doesn't speak, but flings something towards the second guard. A fine powder hits his face, and his skin starts to burn. As he claws at his cheeks, she shoves something into his mouth, then takes a piece of wood and swings it at his head. When it connects with a solid thunk, he crumples into a writhing, wailing ball before his voice fades away completely. Foam forms at the corners of their mouths, and the stench... If I had anything in my stomach, I would vomit.

Straightening, the woman brushes off her hands with a triumphant expression, then rushes over to me.

I don't have the strength to speak. Hell, I can barely hold my head up. She reaches into her pocket, and when she pulls her hand out and unfurls her fingers, I blink hard to focus.

Iron shavings.

"Is...Aurelia...?"

The woman places other hand over my heart for a moment

and nods, then sprinkles some of the shavings over the collar around my neck.

Pure agony sears my skin, and my vision goes white, but the next thing I know, my dragon whimpers, and I sense him deep inside me. He is weak. In pain. As close to death as he can be—while still being immortal—but present.

The woman is behind me. I can feel her dress brush my naked ass and her hands on the collar.

The charmed metal falls to the floor, and the beast inside me roars to life. My bones break, stretch, and reform, scales cover my skin, and a burst of fire leaves my lips and incinerates the bodies of the two guards.

The woman gasps from behind me as I break the shackles around my wrists and ankles, then send my dragon to rest as my human side takes control. My body is still weak, and I stumble off the bloody dais. My rescuer catches me before I hit the ground, and her cheeks flame as I am still completely naked. I have no idea what those fools did with my clothing.

"I will not harm you," I say, my voice hoarse and broken, foreign to my own ears.

She steadies me, then backs away, glancing at the door as if she fears more guards will soon come. But then, she reaches into a small bag at her hip and pulls out a flask. Pantomiming that I am to drink, she thrusts it into my hands.

"You are not Fae." I grasp her wrist and stare into her eyes. One of them bears a fading bruise at least week old, and her entire lower jaw is swollen. Under my fingers, her skin bears old scars—and fresh abrasions—and I shift my grip slightly so I do not hurt her. "Who are you?"

She touches her fingers to her lips, then opens her mouth, and I understand.

"The Prince?" A shake of her head. "The King, then." A nod,

and she gestures for me to drink again. "Is this charmed?" I ask, still holding on to her.

Another shake of her head and the look on her face tells me whatever this is will not harm me, so I let her go, pull the stopper, and down the entire contents in two swallows.

Almost immediately, my body feels stronger. "Thank you. I need clothing and Aurelia. Do you know where she is?"

This beaten, mute, human woman may be my only hope of finding my mate, and my dragon is still too weak to help me. Holding out her hand, she waits for me to link our fingers, and then leads me from the room.

By the top of the first set of stairs, my legs shake with each step, and the woman slips my arm over her shoulders. Faint footsteps head towards us, and I tense. "Someone comes," I whisper. My senses are always heightened, even when my dragon is dormant, which has saved my life more than once.

She pulls me around a corner and shoves me into an alcove where I crouch behind her. She is almost skeletal, and her gown will not hide me, but if she can distract the Fae approaching for even a moment, I might be able to subdue him.

My beast resists my call. He fears the pain of being collared once more.

"If you do not lend me your strength, we will surely die."

He whines, but pushes himself close to the surface. Five talons lengthen from my fingers, and I pray I will be able to fight.

"What are you doing here?" an angry male voice demands, and the woman makes a loud, unintelligible vocalization and points down the hall away from the stairs. "Wait!" She's flung aside by the guard, and I spring for the bastard who sent her crashing into the opposite wall. My talons rake across his throat, tearing out his windpipe with a single swipe, and though this is not enough to kill him, it does silence him.

The woman crawls over with something clutched in her hand. Wrenching the Fae's mouth open, she shoves the small, dark object inside, and he writhes, a terrible hissing and bubbling sound coming from his mouth.

When he breathes no more, I stare up at her, and she shows me two of the iron studs from my belt. "You found my bag."

She smiles, then jerks her head in the direction the Fae came from. Her eyes are bright, and hope burns within their green depths. "I trust you, human. If we survive the day, perhaps we will all manage to be free of this place forever."

I lean heavily on her, trying to conserve my strength, and after another two long flights of stairs, she pulls me into a lavish suite of rooms. They smell like her, and she brings me to a four-poster bed and lets me sit while she goes to the closet along one wall.

Shackles hang from each of the posters, and there is a smear of blood on the polished wood floor next to the bed. She has been tortured in this room. I see it in her eyes when she turns back to me and holds a cloak in one hand and a sheet in the other.

"Good enough," I say as I fasten the cloak around my neck. I do not bother with the sheet. It would only hinder my movements. "Can you write? Communicate in any way beyond yes and no? I believe you may have the one answer I need to get us all out of here."

Trepidation churns in her green gaze.

"Please. Aurelia is trapped her by her bargain with the King, and if she cannot utter the Prince's name—his true name—the King's charm will kill her if she tries to leave. She is my mate. If you can tell me his name, I can get her out of this place. And we will free you as well."

After a hard swallow, the woman drops to her knees and reaches under the bedside table. She withdraws several scraps of paper, a fountain pen, and a jar of ink—nearly empty.

Her hand shakes as she writes, and she has to stop three times to take deep, shuddering breaths before she passes me a scrap of paper.

I can never leave. Too many bargains laid on top of one another. Nor can I give you what you need. The King forced me to agree if I even thought my son's name again, the pain...

She winces and collapses in a heap. Carefully, I gather her into my arms and lay her on the bed before brushing her hair away from her face. "You have freed me. That is more than I could ever have asked—ever have expected. Do you have any more of those iron studs?"

Though her movements are slow and clumsy, and she wavers when she sits up, she nods.

Six left. I tuck them into the pockets of the cloak and take her hand. "If we kill the King, all of your bargains...they disappear. Come with me. Perhaps we will find a way."

With a decisive nod, she lets me help her to her feet, and together, we steal back into the halls.

"*Find our mate,*" I tell the beast inside me. "*Do it now.*"

He roars in my head, a battle cry I know well. He will not fail.

CHAPTER FOURTEEN

AURELIA

Despite the remnants of my corset and skirt lying atop the hay, my boots are nowhere to be found. So, barefoot, I creep down the stairs one floor at a time, letting my instincts guide me. My new-found powers are growing, and my skin tingles. The voices in my head—the Fae voices—ebb and flow, and I have to focus to make one at a time stand out amid the din.

Thoughts about the impending Market day. About the King's treatment of his *consort*. About the Prince's change in temperament after my arrival.

Nothing about my escape or Roarke. Not until I reach a hallway with thick rugs and paintings in gilded frames. The air here is colder, more sinister, and the King's thoughts float into my head.

"The dragon's power is better than the finest wine. I want to see how close to death we can take him. It is possible he will give us so much power, we will be unable to absorb it all."

I cover my mouth to stop my gasp.

"Father," the Prince says, "I do not think I should wait to wed Lia. She is stronger than either of us thought. She has not agreed, but with the dragon in our control, we can trick her into another bargain. She has already agreed to bind herself to me if we let him go."

"I am never releasing the dragon," the King replies mildly, as if he is discussing whether or not to toss a feather upon the wind, not a majestic creature he has chained and close to death. "I have grown fond of his delicious energy."

I tiptoe closer, my bare feet making no sound on the thick rugs. Risking a single glance around a corner, I try to memorize the layout of the room. The King and the Prince sit facing the hearth, each with a glass of amber liquid in their hands.

With shrug, the Prince says, "There is no need to release him. I have spent the past few hours thinking of the perfect bargain to make with my sweet bride."

"Tell me, son." The King sets his glass down and leans forward, and I can hear the excitement and pride in his voice. Sick bastard.

"I will tell her that we will let the dragon walk out of the castle. Unaccompanied. No Fae will follow him. But we will take his voice so that he can never speak ill of us. She must agree to marry me as soon as he leaves. I will even allow her to watch him go free." The Prince takes another sip of his drink as the King frowns.

"If we let him leave, he will be able to shift. To escape," the King says.

The Prince chuckles. "Hardly. We will provide him clothing and use our glamour to hide the collar around his neck. And without his tongue, he will never be able to tell Lia what we have done."

"He could still hide from us."

With a wave of his hand, the Prince dismisses his father's concern. "I have two magic-bearers bound to me. They will follow the dragon, and as soon as he is out of Lia's sight, they will trap him and return him to the castle. She will never know, and even if one day, I decide to punish her and show her how we have destroyed everything he is, there is no lie. Nothing that nullifies our bargain."

"And by then..." the King adds, "you will have broken her as I have broken my human toy."

Tears burn my eyes, but I will not let them fall. Anger flares white hot, and I am about to creep closer when strong arms grab me and propel me forward.

"My liege, I found her in the hall," the guard says as I struggle to escape his hold.

The King and the Prince leap up, and the hatred in the Prince's eyes...it terrifies me more than anything he has done to me thus far. The dagger is still strapped to my thigh, and I tore a slit in the white silk gown to allow myself easy access to the blade, but the guard has my hands pinned behind my back, and he is crushing my broken fingers. The pain is almost too much for me to remain standing.

"Well, well, sweet Lia. How did you free yourself from those chains?" the Prince asks as he grabs my chin and forces me to meet his gaze. I will my mind to go blank, but I must not be quick enough, because he snorts and arches a brow at his father. "My whore mother released her."

"Guards!" The King's call echoes throughout the room, and three more Fae rush in. "Find my consort and bring her to me. Do not be gentle."

"No! Do not punish her!" I cry, and the guard holding me squeezes my wrists and hands tighter. My knees buckle, and I hit the ground, hard.

"Do you think you have any power here, Lia?" the Prince

asks. "Hardly. You do not demand. You do not even ask for a *thing* in my presence. I own you."

"Take me to see Roarke," I sob as fat tears spill down my cheeks. "I beg you. One kindness. I will never ask for another."

I need him to see that I have broken completely. That he has won. Only then will he let down his defenses at all. The guard no longer holds me, and I crawl towards the Prince's feet, lowering my head to the ground and kissing his soft slipper. "I will be yours. I could have run. Instead, I came to find you. I only wish to say goodbye."

His laugh makes my blood run cold. "I would have liked to see you try and escape. You are bound to this castle. Or have you forgotten?"

"There are hundreds of places to hide within these walls," I say, peering up at him through my curtain of black hair.

He considers this, then glances at his father. I fill my mind with images of a binding ceremony. I stand at the Prince's side, not smiling, but not fighting as the King loops a piece of black silk around our joined hands. The thoughts make me want to vomit, but I have to hold my true feelings in check.

"Very well. I suppose if we wed now, I will not have to wait so long to have you. But you will be punished thoroughly for what you have done this day."

"Thank you," I choke out, then hold out my left hand, hoping he will help me to my feet. If I kill him, the bargain will be null and void, and I will be able to escape this place. Once I find Roarke. At least...I hope.

As the Prince grabs my elbow, I hear his thoughts. He's practically singing to himself.

"Such games I play. Clever, clever, Rumpelstiltskin. I will have endless fun with her. And when she is mine, I will make her say my name over and over and over again, just so I can torture her with it. Once we are bound, it will do her no good."

I only have a second to revel in the joy of my new-found powers before the Prince—Rumpelstiltskin—shoves me at his father. I reach for the blade strapped to my thigh. The shock of the iron in my hand throws me off balance, but I manage to drive the dagger into the King's side. He lets out a hoarse cry, and as his body starts to fall, he grabs me around the waist and takes me down with him.

"Iron," he manages as I twist the dagger and try to wrench it free, but his hold on me is too strong. I have no leverage.

The Prince spits out a few words in his native tongue, and the air leaves the room with a great *whoosh*. I start to choke and panic, but keep my fingers tight around the hilt of the weapon as the guard grabs my hair and yanks me back. With what might be my last act before I pass out, I slash at the tall, lanky Fae and open a cut on his thigh.

"Stop!"

Roarke. His voice in my head gives me a burst of strength, though when I look up, he clutches his throat, the Prince's charm extending far enough to affect him as well.

"You can do this, Aurelia. Call for air."

I concentrate on that one word. Air. The breath I draw is too thin, too small. But it is not nothing. Holding onto that thought as long as I can, I manage another. Then another, but a dozen guards rush the man I love, tackling him and sending him to the ground. The Prince releases his charm, flooding the room with so much air, it stings my eyes and cheeks, blistering my skin.

I stagger to my feet as a great roar comes from under the pile of Fae. The sound turns into a growl, and then a burst of fire hits the ceiling. I hear a muffled voice in my head. *"Aurelia, get down..."*

Hitting the floor and taking the guard with me, I struggle as flames shoot across the room and singe the Prince's tunic.

He's distracted, even angrier now as he drops and rolls around to dampen the fire, and I drag my blade across the guard's balls, kick him off of me, and lunge for my tormentor. The dagger sinks deep into the Prince's shoulder. I lie on top of him, grinning.

"Rumplestiltskin, I do not want you. I will never love—"

He slaps his hand over my mouth, but I push the blade deeper, and his strength fades. With my knee pressing down on his pathetic cock, I lift myself up high enough he can no longer silence me. "Rumpelstiltskin, you are not as smart or as clever as you think you are. I do not love you and I will never marry you."

His scream is one of pure torment and agony, and I wrench the dagger free from his flesh and then plunge it into his neck, preventing him from uttering another word ever again.

Something crashes against the stone walls, a great presence filling the room, and I stare at my dragon. He is magnificent. Green scales with a golden shine cover his massive body, and his tail swishes once, knocking the three Fae guards still alive into the far wall. Noelle darts forward and shoves something into each of their mouths before they can rise again, and they start to convulse, then lie still.

The beast snorts and paws the floor, leaving deep gouges in the stone with his talons.

Every part of me hurts, but I pull the dagger from the Prince's body and run for my mate. His wing wraps around me, scooping me up and cradling me protectively against his body. His chest is half the size of my entire cottage, and he is so very warm.

"Roarke."

My dragon lets out a possessive growl, then gently sets me down, folds his wings against his back, and bows his head to nuzzle my neck. I stroke his jaw, and his golden eyes meet mine. Even in this form, I see love reflected back at me.

His legs fold, and he starts to shift before my eyes. The process takes long moments, and I keep looking over my shoulder, fearful we will encounter more guards—or worse. Another member of the royal family. Assuming there are any left.

Roarke—the man—falls to his knees in front of me, naked, his chest heaving, and I wrap my arms around him. "Aurelia, we must go. Now. Help me?"

"What is wrong? You are frightening me." The strong, majestic beast is gone, and left in its place is a man who looks like he is about to die.

He cups my cheek, and his lips curve into a smile. "Nothing rest and being free of this place—with my mate—will not fix, darling."

A flash of movement catches my eye from behind him, and I push to my feet, the dagger in my hand. Noelle. She stands behind Roarke with a cape in her hands, gesturing to him. Of course. He's naked.

"Come with us," I say, but she shakes her head, steps closer, and holds out her hand. Roarke pulls the cloak around his body as I lay my fingers over hers. She guides my hand to her forehead, and I do not even need to concentrate to hear her thoughts as clearly as if she were speaking aloud.

"*I have another son. The King locked him away years ago when his powers started to grow beyond Rumpel's. He is a good man. I must find him and free him.*"

I tell Roarke what she says, and he pushes to his feet with a groan. "Will he harm the people of this realm?"

Noelle shakes her head. "*No. Adrian's powers have been... bound. Even if what has taken place this day restores them...I know his heart. He will never harm another.*"

The Prince makes a gurgling sound from across the room, and Noelle's stare hardens. She pulls a small piece of iron from a pouch at her hip. I can sense it, and I take a step back.

Stalking over to her son, she shoves the piece of iron into the wound at his neck, and his body starts convulsing as she rests her hands on her hips. Next, she turns to the King. He does not move, even after her single, well-placed kick. Noelle she huffs, then glances at us and nods. The King and the Prince are dead.

My bargain with them is broken, and I am finally free.

CHAPTER FIFTEEN

ROARKE

"Aurelia, I need you." Some of my deeper wounds have started to bleed once more, and I am weakening. My dragon demands to be released, but I fear if I let him out, shifting back might kill us both.

I ease the dagger from her hand as I drape my other arm over her slight shoulders. She should not have to bear my weight, but she is stronger than I ever knew. Watching her pull air back into the room after the Prince used his charms was the sexiest, most powerful display of magic I have ever seen outside of shifting.

Two Fae round the corner, and I brandish the dagger as I shout, "Out of our way. Do not make me end you."

"The King is dead," one of them says. His glamour falls away, and the tall, broad-shouldered male shrinks before my eyes. He is a head shorter than I am, with spindly arms and legs and a young, fresh face. "We felt it. We have been trapped here for centuries and now...we are free."

Aurelia looks from the two Fae to me and back again. "You were trapped...?"

"Not all Fae are like he was. Some of us seek nothing but a peaceful existence among humans or a return to the Fae realm. When the King was banished centuries ago, he set a trap. More than half of the Fae in this castle did not choose to come here. Now, we are free. I miss my home. My family back in the Fae realm."

My mate sucks in a sharp breath. "We...can leave this realm?"

"I do not know how the King created this place. The Fae have their own plane of existence and should never have claimed part of this world," I say.

"The King's magic is gone. And with it the veil that separated us from the rest of the earth. Go," the guard says and bows before Aurelia. "We know what the Prince planned for you, and we vow—on our immortal souls—to protect you for as long as we live. Both of you."

"You know what I am," I say. It is not a question, and trepidation tightens in my gut. The Fae and the dragons are mortal enemies. I have too much power inside my beast for us to be anything else.

"We do, shifter." The other guard, who is shorter than the first, nods. His tone is not entirely friendly, but he too bows. "We have taken from the unwilling for too long. The power is bitter. Harsh. I would rather languish and pass into the afterlife than sustain myself on it any longer. If we cannot return to our own realm, I can think of no better penance than to entomb ourselves in the rubble of this tower. We can destroy it. Once the human and the tortured prince are free, we will do that very thing."

Aurelia tightens her arm around my waist. "I believe them, Roarke. They are not evil, even if they have done evil things."

"Very well. But I am keeping the dagger close," I say as the guards press themselves against the wall to allow us to pass.

Aurelia supports more and more of my weight as we descend the stairs, and when we reach the door that leads outside, she hesitates. "What if...?"

"You said his name, my love. You told him you would never love him."

"But—"

I silence her with my kiss, and a burst of strength infuses my limbs. She is perfection. Her taste like the sweetest fruit, like the wind as my dragon flies free and unburdened, like pure sunshine. Taking her moan of pleasure within me, I let her feel the hard length of my cock against her belly, and the scent of her arousal swirls around me.

"I will not let anything happen to you, Aurelia. If the worst comes to pass, we will find a way to break the charm. Together."

Her lips are swollen from our shared passion, and her eyes sparkle in the afternoon sunlight. With her pressed to my side, we take a single step onto the thick carpet of moss outside the tower, and Aurelia breathes deeply.

"I..." Tears tumble from her eyes, and she throws her arms around me and holds on like she may never let go.

Strong enough now, I scoop her up and cradle her to my chest. "Come home with me, mate. Your father is safe with a friend of mine, and I...need to rest with you in my arms. After that, if the barrier truly has been broken, we can go anywhere you wish and start a new life. Together."

Rolling over, I stifle my groan. My injuries—those that remain —are healing, but the memory of the Fae's torture will never fade. Beside me, Aurelia sleeps soundly. I fashioned a splint for her broken fingers, and when we mate, our bond will give her some of my strength—enough to mend the shattered bones at least.

She and her father had a stilted reunion. Keeping the secret of her true parentage from her... I was not certain she would forgive him. I never will. But they embraced before Crux allowed him to return to his cottage, and she promised we would not leave without saying goodbye.

The veil hiding this realm from the rest of the world has fallen, and many of the outcasts have already left. Those who stepped into the Fae's charmed circle less than ten years ago were the first to go. We saw several of them carrying small sacks of their belongings and running into the forest as we made our way to my home.

"Roarke?"

Her voice soothes me, and I brush a lock of hair away from her face. "Yes, my love?"

"This is a dream." Her eyes shimmer with unshed tears, and I cup her cheek and brush my thumb over her lips.

"No, Aurelia. This is no dream." I cannot keep a hint of sadness from my voice as I gently lift her hand to examine her broken fingers. "In a dream, we would be whole."

She feathers a touch over a healing patch of skin along my side. One of my larger...*offerings* to the King. That wound gave him so much power, he could no longer walk a straight line.

"Will we ever be whole again?" she asks.

"We are together. Does anything else matter?" Leaning in, I press a chaste kiss to her lips. "You did not get to see the best part of this house last night. May I show you?"

She nods, and with our arms around one another, we shuffle into the bathroom. I worked for years on this room. In one corner, there is a lavish teak wood sauna, and in the other, a shower large enough for the both of us.

"Is there...*warm* water?" Aurelia asks.

"My love...when you are with a dragon, there is always hot water. The boiler in back of the house took me decades to perfect. Wait here?" I ease her down onto the bench in the sauna, but her eyes widen, and she shakes her head.

"No. I want to stay with you. Please, Roarke."

I should not have been so thoughtless. She has no cause to fear. Not now. But nor do I, and my nightmares woke me several times during the night. "Of course, my love."

Leading her outside, I warn her to stay back, then let my dragon take control. The shift is only partial, just enough for him to call forth the flames that turn the metal of the boiler red hot.

Aurelia gasps, and I cut my gaze to her, worried I've somehow frightened her, but instead, she watches in awe. "You are magnificent," she breathes, and my dragon preens as he retreats back to his dormancy.

Her body is bruised from her shoulders to her feet, and out here, in the daylight, the black, blue, and purple marks look so much worse. "Let me care for you," I say as I move to scoop her up into my arms. But she takes a step back, her hands raised.

"N-no. That's what... He said that before he...bathed me. I was so confused then. I thought—for a few moments--that he was not a monster. He addled my mind." A shudder runs through her entire body, and I curse myself for not doing something to stop her from making that bargain in the first place. It matters not that Crux and Valinor were holding me. I should have shifted, released my dragon, the Fae be damned.

I do not know what to say or do, but my mate is stronger than I ever suspected. She covers her face with her hands for a moment, then takes a deep breath. "I am sorry, Roarke. I know you are not him. Can we perhaps try this again?"

Wrapping my arms around her, I nuzzle her neck, the urge to bite her, to give her my mark and claim her as mine forever, so strong, I can barely stand it. But she is not ready yet. She may never be. Not after what she endured. And I will wait, by her side, or close, for as long as she needs.

"I love you," she whispers.

"And I love you." Hand in hand, we walk back inside, and I gesture to the shower. "Let me show you how to work this."

I expect her to ask me to leave, despite the fact that we slept naked in each other's arms all night, but as she steps under the spray, she holds out her hand. "Will you join me?"

"Aurelia, I would do anything for you."

THREE DAYS PASS, and we still have not mated. But Aurelia smiles often, laughs, and sleeps against me each night. We spend our time getting to know one another in every way. All the ways we should have *before* these horrors. If only I had not been so afraid of the Fae noticing me, we could have been mated years ago.

On the third night, when we climb into bed, she pulls me close. "Roarke? I have never felt like this before. It is as if my heart beats only for you."

"That is as it should be. As it always is for those who are fated to love one another," I say.

"But how do you know this? Until a few days ago, I thought I was human. We do not...mate. We form partnerships. We marry. Sometimes, there is even love involved. But we do not simply 'find our mate.'"

"This is the blessing of being *other*. Shifters, Fae, even

witches feel this pull, from what I have always been taught. My parents...their souls were intertwined. So much so that they died within minutes of one another."

She covers her mouth with her hand, but I shake my head. "No, my love. That is how they wished it to be. They were never parted. Not even in death."

Aurelia is silent for long moments, then, in the waning light, she leans up on an elbow so her hair hangs down and tickles my shoulder. "I have never...been with a man. But these past days, being so close to you, I want you, Roarke. I want you for the rest of my days. I *need* you. And as ridiculous as this sounds, I need you to claim me."

Carefully, I ease her on top of me so she can feel the hard length of my cock. It weeps for her, only for her, and Aurelia shifts her hips against me.

"Fuck, Aurelia. My love. My heart and soul."

She peers down at me with hooded eyes. "Tell me what to do."

"Lie back and let yourself feel."

Making herself comfortable on the bed, she watches me as I part her legs and position myself between them.

"Roarke? What are you doing?"

"Oh, my love, there is so much more to sex than...the single act you have imagined." I smile up at her, my hands caressing her creamy skin. "If you need me to stop, you have only to say."

The dewy curls covering her mound beckon me, and I plant gentle kisses from her knee to the junction of her thighs, and with every one, she trembles.

Down the other leg, back up again, and her hips start to have a mind of their own.

"I am going to taste you now, my love."

Aurelia tenses, but when my tongue parts her slick folds, she cries out in pleasure. "Roarke! What...? I..."

Crawling up her body, I silence her cries with a kiss, then once she is panting, her unbroken fingers digging into my back, I score my teeth over one dusky pink nipple, and she shudders, her back arching.

"I cannot be selfish," I whisper against her other breast, and by the time I kiss my way back down her stomach and to her mound, she's babbling incoherently. I catch the occasional word.

"Need."

"More."

"Oh!"

My second taste is more delicious than the first, and I lap at her essence, finding the tiny nub that will undo her. Feet scrambling for purchase against the sheets, she cries out, louder now, and I think I hear my name, but I focus only on Aurelia. On sending her over the edge and into an ocean of pleasure.

"WHAT...WAS...THAT?" she manages after her tremors subside. I have her in my arms, the blankets drawn up over her shoulders. My dragon warms us from within, and my teeth ache with the need to claim her fully—to mark her.

"That was only the beginning." Our kiss tastes of her pleasure, and she skims her uninjured hand down my abs until she finds the hard length of my cock.

Now, it is my turn to shudder and groan. I have wanted this for so very long, and the idea that I almost lost her—that we almost lost each other—is too much to bear. "I love you, Aurelia. I want to make you mine. Forever. But only if you want that as well."

With her fingers still wrapped around my shaft, she meets

my gaze. "I have known since the moment in the square. When I saw your eyes as the King bound me. I knew you loved me then. And that I felt the same."

Hope fills my heart. "Does that mean...?"

"Yes, Roarke. I want to be yours, and I will make you mine. Tell me what to do." Positioning myself over her, I nudge at her entrance, and her eyes widen. "Will it hurt?"

"Only for a moment." I seal my promise with a kiss, and she wraps her legs around my hips, welcoming me home.

A single gasp escapes her lips when I push past her barrier, and then, she draws me deep, her eyes open, her gaze locked on mine. "I do not know how the Fae claim their mates. Or if they even do. But I claim you, Roarke. My dragon. I name you the keeper of my heart, the guardian of my soul."

Aurelia places her fingers over my heart, and for a single moment, white hot pain sears my skin. But it fades almost immediately as she jerks her hand away with a tiny mewl. "I marked you," she says with wonder.

The brand is the most stunning mark I have ever seen. My dragon flies, wings spread, with a silhouette of Aurelia perched on his back. The design is small. No larger than her palm, but exquisitely detailed, and there is no question it is the two of us.

"I did not know I could do that," she says. "There is something you must do to claim me? I can feel it. This overwhelming *need* deep inside me. I will not be complete without—"

With a growl, I lunge forward and clamp my teeth around the soft skin at the curve of her neck. Aurelia whimpers as her core tightens around me, and when my dragon's fangs descend and break the skin, she cries out in pleasure. I thrust hard and deep, and Aurelia's short nails dig into my back. My new brand presses to her breast, and we are connected in every possible way as we lose ourselves to our shared pleasure.

CHAPTER SIXTEEN

AURELIA

Roarke tells me of the world outside the realm, and though I fear the unknown, I do not wish to stay here. There are too many memories.

The castle fell two days after we escaped. The ground shook, and we ran outside to see the stones crumbling in on themselves. The guards did as they promised, and I cannot help but hope they found their way home.

"How will we survive?" I ask as I pack up the last of my meager belongings. I own little beyond the wool, cotton, and silk garments I spun myself. My mother's golden hairpins, my grandmother's locket, and the iron dagger that saved our lives. Roarke wrapped it in several thick pieces of leather so it would not harm me, but I can still sense it, even now.

"Dragons," he says with a smile, "are hoarders. Bright, shiny objects, stores of food, and money. I have been gone for many years, but some of my stores should remain. And if not, we will find my brothers. They will shelter us until we decide where in this vast world we wish to go."

"They will not hate me?" I rub my fist against my heart. This power inside me still feels foreign, and it aches when I focus on it.

"You are my mate. They could not hate you. Not ever." He slides his arm around my back and pulls me close. "Dragons and the Fae have been enemies for thousands of years. We can change that."

Wrapping a large piece of leather around his trunk, he tests the knots, nods, and then hefts the trunk onto his back. I follow him outside into the morning sun, and frown. "What are you doing?"

"Aurelia, my love," he says as he loosens two buttons on his silk shirt and shows me the brand I gave him during our mating, "the fastest way to reach Alaska is to fly."

Ducking into his cottage quickly, he returns with a long, leather coat and thick pair of gloves and holds them out for me. "These will keep you warm."

"And you?" I ask, eyeing his bare feet and half-buttoned shirt.

Roarke grins as he strips off his clothing, folds the pants and shirt, and tucks them into a bag secured to the trunk. I watch, transfixed, as his dragon emerges. He is pure power and grace, and the magic rolling off of him glows and makes his scales shimmer.

One wing angles down to the ground, and I can hear him in my head, telling me how to mount him and where to hold on.

"Are you ready, my love?" Roarke asks as he grasps the leather cord in his talons and lifts his massive head.

"Y-yes." In truth, I do not believe anything could prepare me for what we are about to do, but he takes several quick steps and flaps his wings, and then there is nothing but the wind on my cheeks and the feel of my dragon beneath me.

I hold onto his neck, his warmth protecting me as we fly faster and higher than I ever imagined. I know the instant we pass what used to be the edge of the realm, and the feeling of pure freedom is one I will relish for a thousand lifetimes.

Excitement makes my heart pound, and I cannot wait to see where he takes us—where life takes us—for an eternity.

THANK you for reading Twisted Captive. Turn the page for an exclusive bonus scene/extended epilogue about Adrian's rescue.

RESCUING ADRIAN

ADRIAN

I sense the moment the King dies. The charms keeping me in constant agony, tormented and unable to speak, to sleep, to find a moment's peace fall away, and my eyes close on a sigh.

Perhaps now, I will die. As half-Fae, I should be immortal, but my *father* and *brother* have kept me chained to this altar in the deepest bowels of the castle for more than a century.

The iron shackles burn my wrists, ankles, and neck every second of every day, and the platform I lie on has an intricate pattern of the deadly metal inlaid into the stone.

A drop of water falls from an iron spike driven into the stone ceiling, right onto my lips, and I force myself to lick it off. Fae can live without food, but the half-human side of me needs water. My sadistic father devised a way to make each drop cause me the maximum amount of pain.

I have no voice. I cannot even moan. He took that from me as well. All because I wished to live among the humans. Because I begged him to free my mother. Because I bested my brother—Rumpel was always my father's favorite—and knocked him down a flight of stairs in the process.

Another drop of water hits my chapped and blistered lips, and the pain sends me into blessed oblivion for the first time in more than two hundred years.

~

The scraping of heavy stone rouses me from unconsciousness. Light sears my eyes, more painful than the iron, than the forced immobility, than the all abiding loneliness that has been my only companion.

"My liege."

I have been trapped in this never-ending silence for so long, I forgot what voices sound like, and this male's call hurts my ears. I wonder if my own vocal cords still function.

A warm hand caresses my arm, then my jaw. I know this touch. This scent. It is one of comfort. Of my childhood. Of love.

Mother?

Tears fall over my cheeks. Her tears. I am so cold, they feel as if they are burning me, and I flinch.

Shock steals my breath. I have not been allowed even that much movement since the King locked me down here.

"My king," the male voice says again, softer this time. "It will take some time to free you. But we will free you."

King?

My mother brings something soft to my lips—a sponge maybe—and liquid flows over them. Pure, untainted water. Not too much. Just enough for me to open my eyes to slits. She has aged in the centuries I have been bound. But thanks to my father's Fae magic, not as much as she should have.

Say something. Please.

I have not heard her voice in so long. But she shakes her head and touches her lips. He silenced her as well. My powers are almost gone. Stolen by iron, starvation, and the King's charms. I cannot read her thoughts. But her emotions overwhelm me. Sadness. Joy. Hope. She gestures at the guard who is working to unlock the iron around my right ankle, then motions for him to speak.

I do not know this male. Or, if I do, I cannot remember him.

"The King and the Prince were banished from the Fae realm, my liege. Fifty human years after they trapped you here. They convinced many of us to join them. But once they sealed off this new realm…" He shakes his head. "They toyed with the humans. Trapped more every full moon."

My father was a monster.

The first shackle cracks open, but the poisonous metal was locked so tight for so long, that it has almost become a part of my ankle.

"This will hurt, my liege."

I cannot nod or speak to give him permission. But I hold his gaze until he pulls the cuff free, tearing my skin off with it.

"It is better this way, my queen. When he wakes, we will be done, and he can start to heal."

I am awake, you dolt. Simply too weak to open my eyes.

My mother makes a low, sorrowful sound and rests her cheek on my shoulder. Again and again, the guard rips off the manacles, until he unlocks the one at my neck. This one…I fear it may kill me.

Forcing my eyes open, I beg him silently. Do not do this. I will bear the pain and the weakness from the iron for the rest of my days—however long they may be—to avoid what I know will be pure agony.

"I am sorry, my liege. But the castle will soon be destroyed, along with all of us who carried out your father's vile deeds.

You and the queen cannot be here when that happens. You deserve to be free." The guard takes a piece of leather from the pocket of his robes and gently guides it between my teeth. "Bite down."

My mother holds my hand, now bloody from the torn skin at my wrist. I must have passed out for at least a short time, for I do not remember the guard moving my arms to my sides—an event I am fortunate I did not have to experience. Bound spread-eagled for centuries, I can only imagine how my joints have locked up and frozen.

This, though...the removal of the collar...this is easier. Perhaps swallowing—the only movement outside of blinking and breathing I was allowed—kept the metal from fusing to my skin.

Tell me more. Please.

My gaze pings from the guard to my mother, and he nods. My own powers are useless, but his...he can understand me.

"The King trapped a human woman in a bargain. Rumpelstiltskin wanted her as his bride. He tortured her, but they—the human and her dragon mate—killed the king and the prince and escaped. But not before the king removed the queen's tongue for speaking out against what he was doing."

Anger flares as I find my mother's eyes filled with tears.

"They are both dead now, my liege. You will be welcomed back in the Fae realm. You and the queen. There...perhaps you will be able to heal."

ABOUT THE AUTHOR

Patricia D. Eddy writes romance for the beautifully broken. Fueled by coffee, wine, and Doctor Who episodes on repeat, she brings damaged heroes and heroines together to find their happy ever afters in many different worlds. From military to paranormal to BDSM, her characters are unstoppable forces colliding with such heat, sparks always fly.

Patricia makes her home in Seattle with her husband and very spoiled cats, and when she's not writing, she loves working on home improvement projects, especially if they involve power tools.

Her award-winning *Away From Keyboard* series will always be her first love, because that's where she realized the characters in her head were telling their own stories—and she was just writing them down.

You can reach Patricia all over the web...
patriciadeddy.com
patricia@patriciadeddy.com

facebook.com/patriciadeddyauthor

twitter.com/patriciadeddy

instagram.com/patriciadeddy

bookbub.com/profile/patricia-d-eddy

Also by Patricia D. Eddy

AWAY FROM KEYBOARD

Dive into a steamy mix of geekery and military prowess with the men and women of Hidden Agenda and Second Sight.

Breaking His Code

In Her Sights

On His Six

Second Sight

By Lethal Force

Fighting For Valor

Finding Their Forevers (a holiday short story)

Call Sign: Redemption

Braving His Past

Protecting His Target

Defending His Hope

Trusting His Instincts

GONE ROGUE (AN AWAY FROM KEYBOARD SPINOFF SERIES)

Rogue Protector

Rogue Officer

Rogue Survivor

Rogue Defender

DARK PNR

These novellas will take you into the darker side of the paranormal with vampires, witches, angels, demons, and more.

Forever Kept

Immortal Hunter

Wicked Omens

Twisted Captive

Storm of Sin

BY THE FATES

Check out the COMPLETE By the Fates series if you love dark and steamy tales of witches, devils, and an epic battle between good and evil.

By the Fates, Freed

Destined: A By the Fates Story

By the Fates, Fought

By the Fates, Fulfilled

IN BLOOD

If you love hot Italian vampires and and a human who can hold her own against beings far stronger, then the In Blood series is for you.

Secrets in Blood

Revelations in Blood

HOLIDAYS AND HEROES

Beauty isn't only skin deep and not all scars heal. Come swoon over sexy vets and the men and women who love them.

Mistletoe and Mochas

Love and Libations

RESTRAINED

Do you like to be tied up? Or read about characters who do? Enjoy a fresh COMPLETE BDSM series that will leave you begging for more.

In His Silks

Christmas Silks

All Tied Up For New Year's

In His Collar